A SIMPLE COUNTRY TRAGEDY

BLYTHE BAKER

~

All the secrets Helen Lightholder has been working to uncover are about to be revealed, as Helen travels to London. Seeking out a colleague of her late husband's, she delves into a murky world of spies and treason, becoming entangled in a web of danger and intrigue.

Meanwhile, dark happenings back in Bookminster end with the murder of a local man. Once again, Helen is called upon to assist Inspector Graves in an investigation, but can she focus on the present when the mysteries of her past beckon?

~

The mist clung to the ground like a blanket of snow. Trees protruded from its depths, like skeletal hands reaching out of a restless grave. Hills disappeared into the low hanging clouds as if they were the tallest of mountains.

The earth was still, apart from the pattering rain and the ripples in the river flowing just outside the village.

I held an umbrella in my hand, staring up the street, waiting for the headlights I knew would come.

Glancing at my watch, I noticed that I only had seven minutes left to wait before the cab arrived...and took me to the destination I was preparing to go to.

"Are you absolutely certain this is what you want to do?"

I turned and saw Irene standing beneath the overhang above my front door. She clutched her shawl more tightly around her shoulders, the chill of the rainy day drawing color to the tip of her nose and fingers.

This woman had been the dearest friend that I'd had since moving to Brookminster. She was kind, patient, and a mother by nature, which left her prone to worrying...even about me.

Her thick, blonde hair was pulled back in a plait she had pinned behind her head with a pretty, shimmering pin. Her grey eyes searched my face, as intently as they always did.

I was convinced more and more that she was more family to me than friend.

"I am," I said. "I've thought about this for nearly three weeks now. I haven't had a proper night's sleep since July."

Irene didn't respond, apart from pulling her shawl more tightly around herself.

My gaze shifted to the other person standing there with us.

Sidney Mason.

Leaning against the door, his blue eyes were downcast on the ground, where puddles were pooling between the cobblestones. His copper hair was growing long around his ears, probably because of the late summer heat. He'd trimmed his beard, too, I noticed. It was much closer to his face, much cleaner looking than even the day before when he'd come to repair the leak in my faucet.

He must have felt my gaze on his face, for he looked up at me, and gave a wry smile. "You know, I feel as if I must agree with Irene in this instance. Are you absolutely certain this is what you want to do? Travel all the way to London... and for what? Just to come home discouraged again?"

Caution was clear in his gaze, and it gave me pause. Sidney was never one for fear or worry, yet ever since I told him that I was going to London to investigate what had happened to Roger, he had been rather distant.

"Yes, what if you don't find the answers you are looking for yet again?" Irene asked. "This man you are meeting, how can you be certain he will be able to do anything to help you?"

"I can't be certain," I said. "But he was one of Roger's oldest friends, and served alongside him since the start of the war. Roger very well may have told him more than he ever told me."

"And what makes you so sure that he will reveal that information to you now?" Sidney asked, his brow furrowing. "Especially if it is some sort of matter of the government?"

I sighed, glancing back down the street. Still no sign of headlights. "I am not sure," I said. "As I have said to you both on more than one occasion now."

"Helen, I understand that you are frightened," Irene said gently. "Anyone would be after having their home broken into so many times – "

"It's not just that, Irene," I said, the raindrops falling off the edge of my umbrella. "It's much more. Whoever it was that was breaking in didn't want anything to do with me. It had everything to do with Roger's things. And I cannot be certain if this person was an enemy or an ally – "

"I thought that would be clear," Sidney said. "Wouldn't it make far more sense for this lunatic to just write you a letter if they were an ally, instead of breaking in and stealing your things to make a point?"

"I suppose," I said. "But it was clearly a warning. Maybe a warning to not forget about Roger. I don't know. I simply cannot shake this feeling that I am just missing something, that everything that's happened isn't finished yet. It cannot be."

"So does this mean that you will leave Brookminster in the end?" Sidney asked.

The weight of his words struck me hard, like a blow to the heart.

I knew that any delay in my response would be as good as admitting I'd considered it, so I could only sigh.

"I don't know what my life holds for me now," I said. "All I do know is that I need answers, about so many things… why Roger died, what was the reason he was killed, and why this person seems so intent on scaring me away from the whole thing."

"But what if this just leads you into danger?" Irene asked. "I cannot think of a clearer message than a shattered picture frame."

I tried to swallow past the lump in my throat. "I need to be brave. I need to stop pretending that Roger's death is over and done with. I know it isn't, and I know there is more to it than what I have been told."

Sidney straightened, moving away from the door, his hands slid deep into his pockets. "Well, Helen, I hope you know there are people here in Brookminster who really care a great deal about you. We only worry because we want you to have a full and happy life…and all this business with Roger just seems so unnecessary."

A twinge of anger rippled through me, but I quickly pushed it aside. He was saying these things out of affection, not out of malice. "I understand," I said. "And I care about you both, as well. But you must understand this about me. I *must* do this. If I don't, then it will come after me all on its own. The only way for me to stop everything that's happening is to confront it, and fight back. Otherwise I will be nothing more than a victim to all this nonsense for the rest of my days."

Irene nodded slowly. "And we do realize that. We only wish we could do something to help you."

"Yes, and we wish we could protect you in some way from all this," Sidney added.

"What would I have you do, hmm?" I asked. "Stand guard outside my door at all hours of the day to ensure the burglar never returned? Should I have bars fixed to my windows? Move across town? No, this person is determined to find something, and my intent is to find it before they do."

Bright lights up ahead on the road caught my attention, drawing my eyes from the front garden to the wet, gleaming street. The lights grew as they drew nearer.

"That'll be George," Irene said behind me, with a tone of defeat.

"Yes, I suppose it is," I said.

The cab pulled up outside the low, stone garden wall. The headlights seemed to flicker as the rain fell straight into their long, narrow beams.

The man who stepped out from the driver's side was a rather husky sort of man, with a broad jaw, and long, drooping jowls that reminded me of a basset hound. "'Ello, dear sister," he said, grinning a toothy smile.

"Hello, George," Irene said, walking out from under the overhang to stand beneath the umbrella with me. "Thank you for coming at such short notice."

"It's not a problem, love, not a problem," said George. He glanced back and forth between Irene and I. "Why the long face, lass? She's only going to London for the week."

"Yes, I know," Irene said, and when I looked up at her, I saw a tight, sad smile on her rosy cheeked face. "You take care now, all right? Make sure to call if you need anything."

She gave me a hug, and as she did, my eyes stung with tears. Why did it feel as if I was betraying her in some way?

When she released me, Sidney walked over and stared at me for a few moments. The rain fell upon his shirt, his face, his hair...and he didn't seem to mind.

He was trying to say something to me, standing there in the horrible weather the way he was. I couldn't put my finger on what it was, exactly...but it was clear that he intended to tell me something.

"Have a safe trip," he said, holding his hand out.

I looked from his hand, back up to his handsome face, my heart twisting in my chest.

He smiled, then. A small smile that only turned up the corner of his mouth, but it was one I was familiar with. It put me at ease.

I took his hand, and he squeezed mine tightly.

"I'll watch your house while you're gone, all right?" he asked. "I promise you that it will be safe with me."

"I know it will be," I said. "And I greatly appreciate it."

He released my hand, the warm pressure of his skin on mine disappearing...leaving a hole in my heart.

"Why don't you hand me your suitcase?" George asked. "I'll get it in the boot before it gets soaked."

"And what about you?" I asked, turning around and smiling at Irene's brother. "You seem to be already soaked through, standing there while I'm blabbering on."

"Never you mind," George said as he hoisted my suitcase over the wall and wandered back to the boot.

Irene had returned to the overhang. "I'll make sure Mrs. Georgianna gets her order on Tuesday, all right?"

"Thank you," I said. "And Mrs. Trent might come

looking for some more ribbon. She's like clockwork, every six weeks."

Irene smiled. "There's no sense in dragging out our goodbyes. Off you go. We don't want you missing your train."

I nodded, and walked to the gate, unlatching it as I had so many times before. For some reason, as I pushed it shut, there was a sense of finality about the sound of the metal sliding home into its lock...as if I might not be the same person when I returned.

"Goodbye," I said from the car door. George had already slid inside, waiting quite patiently for me in the front seat.

Both Sidney and Irene waved, though Irene's was far more exuberant than Sidney's.

Irene's right. No sense in dragging this out.

With one last smile at the pair of them, I pulled open the door, shut my umbrella with a snap, and slid inside before the rain could flood the car.

"Very good," said George, smiling over at me. "Off to the station we go, then."

I looked out the window, and saw Irene and Sidney speaking to one another. Irene looked concerned once again, and Sidney shook his head somberly.

My heart sank.

Irene noticed me looking, though, and her smile returned as she waved at me.

I waved back as we pulled away down the street.

Brookminster disappeared quickly as we headed outside the town limits.

"Thank you for coming to pick me up, George," I said. "I know petrol is quite expensive these days."

"It's not a problem, lass," he said, giving me a hearty

wink. I noticed his eyes were the same shade of grey as Irene's. "Believe it or not, there are still many who would rather use a car for transport than walk anywhere, even in a little village like ours."

"I'm not surprised," I said, thinking of Sidney who loved that truck he'd inherited shortly after arriving in Brookminster.

A few moments passed in silence before George broke it with a loud chuckle.

"Do you remember that first day we met?" he asked. "When I picked you up from the station and brought you here to Brookminster?"

I smiled, thinking back on that day. "Yes, I do. You were the first person to show me kindness in Brookminster."

"Aw, don't say that," George said, chuckling. "I'm glad you came, though, Helen. Irene needed someone like you to mother so that she would stop bothering me so much."

He gave me another wink, and I smiled.

"In all seriousness, though, you are just the sort of friend she needed. You've got a little spunk in you. My sister is always such a worry wart. It's good for her to get a little excitement in her life."

*I wonder if he knows what sort of excitement we've been up to...*I thought. Between eavesdropping on criminals and storming the homes of possible murderers, we had likely had more excitement than anyone needed to ever experience in their whole lives.

The train station wasn't nearly as far away as I remembered it being. George and I whittled away the drive by talking about his nephew, Michael, Irene and Nathanial's son, which was quite pleasant.

When we arrived, the storm had only gotten worse, and I feared it might cause the train to be delayed.

"As long as the storm keeps moving west, you should be fine," George said as he carried my suitcase to a trolley just outside the main doorways. "If not, just give Irene a call and she can contact me. I'll come back and get you."

"Thank you, George," I said, and reached into my pocket for the money I owed him.

He held up his hands, backing away into the downpour. "Your money is no good here, lass. You're practically family now."

Even though I was quite flattered, I still felt guilty. "Are you certain? It could cover the cost of some tea when you get back. I wouldn't want you to fall ill because of me."

He shook his head, turning on his heel and hurrying back down the steps. "Have a good trip, Helen. We'll see you when you get back!"

I stood there, money still clutched in my hand, watching him leave.

*I'll just leave some tucked in his glove box when I come back...*I thought as I turned my luggage trolley around and pushed it into the station.

The train to London wasn't canceled, thankfully. I boarded without trouble an hour later, and a few hours after that, watched the city lights appear on the horizon out the window.

I'd been reading the letter in my hand for the third time that trip as the train entered the city, the grandeur of the Thames River glittering in all the lights, reflecting the grey, dark storm clouds above.

The letter held the address of the man I was going to meet. A one Patrick Gordon. I had heard Roger speak of him several times, but could never remember his full name. And with the letters that Roger had written to me stolen, I couldn't refer to them for certainty.

This had led me to seek out the help of Sam Graves, who seemed slightly put out by my request, reminding me that he had things like murders and thefts to be dealing with, but he agreed to help all the same.

To my dismay, there were several Patrick Gordon's in London, but Sam's detective abilities had helped us to narrow down the list to just two possibilities. I sent the same letter to both men. Very short and as cordial as I could be, I asked them if they had been in the military, and if they had been friends with a late Roger Lightholder. I didn't feel comfortable giving any further information than that, just in case the letter was intercepted somewhere.

The first letter I received in return was from someone apologizing, but they had never heard the name before.

Rather discouraged, I began to wonder if I had done nothing but waste my time when a second letter arrived, and was similarly as short.

Helen,

It's wonderful to hear from you. Lily and I had wondered what happened to you after Roger's death. I certainly did know him, and knew him well. I'm sorry that we never had the chance to meet in person, but I am pleased that you reached out to me. How have you been? Have you been able to make any peace with Roger's passing? Awaiting your response at...

His address was listed there, but we had corresponded several more times over the last few weeks. I realized that he spoke in very general terms about Roger and their relationship, so I followed suit. It seemed that my hunch was correct, and that Patrick had been around when Roger had been killed. In his last letter, he asked if I would want to come and stay with him and his family, where we could speak further, perhaps share some happy memories about Roger.

Something within me realized that he was warning me, in a very subtle way, not to say much more in a letter.

I agreed to come meet them, and with that, the hope of learning the truth about what happened to Roger had been reignited within me.

I disembarked the train, glad to see that the rains had finally ceased. The clouds were dark overhead, though, swollen with rain, and I knew it would not be long before they began their deluge once more.

It was quite strange, being back in London. I never thought I would return here. Maybe one day, to pay my respects at Roger's grave...but I was only partially surprised about how morose I was feeling to be back. I felt exposed. Raw. I wanted nothing more than to run and hide.

I flagged down a cab outside the station, and gave the cabbie the address that Patrick had given me.

A little more than a half hour later, I found myself standing outside a charming townhome on a quiet street in north London. A couple walked their dog on the sidewalk across the street, and a horn honked in the distance.

I thanked the cabbie and dragged my suitcase up the steps.

The name *Gordon* was painted on a small plaque just above the black mailbox, which hung beside the door.

I reached out and pressed the doorbell directly below, and heard it sound from somewhere deep within the antiquated building.

Barking answered the chime, which was quickly

followed by a voice. "Coming, coming. Hold on just one moment. Bailey, please."

I heard a lock flip, and the door was pulled open a moment later.

A man who was built incredibly like Roger had been was crouched over, straddling the back of a small horse...no, a hound of some sort.

"Sorry about that," the man said, smiling up at me. "You must be Helen."

2

Patrick Gordon was a handsome man in his mid-forties. He had dark hair that was trimmed the same way Roger's always was, a mark of his service in the military. His eyes were a piercing blue, reminding me of Sam Graves.

He let go of the great, black hound's collar with one hand and held it out to me. "It's nice to finally meet you. I'm Patrick Gordon."

I took his hand and shook, smiling at him. "It's nice to meet you as well. And who is this?"

"Oh, this? Bailey. He's harmless. He likes company just as much as we do," Patrick said.

"Hello, Bailey," I said, allowing him to sniff the back of my fingers. His cool, wet nose tickled, and it drew a genuine smile to my face.

Patrick stood there with his hand on his waist. "He doesn't do much good when it comes to sussing out trouble-makers, though, because all he wants to do is lick their hands and receive the elusive ear pets. Now..." He swung his leg back over the dog, and gave him an affectionate bop on the rear. "Off you go, Bailey. Let the poor woman inside."

Bailey turned around, very much like a horse, and lumbered back out of sight.

Patrick grinned at me, and stooped to take my suitcase from my hand. "Please, come in. The last thing I'd want is for you to get caught in the rain."

"Thank you very much," I said.

He stood aside and allowed me to pass through the door.

Their home was charming. An antique rug lined the front hall, and an old train lantern hung just inside the door, illuminating the space. Paintings of the countryside hung on the walls, and a coat rack behind the door revealed both adults and children's jackets, all of which appeared to be damp with rain still.

"Honey, is that her?" came a woman's voice down the hall.

"Yes, dear," said Patrick, smiling at me and waving to follow. "All the way from Gloucestershire."

A woman leaned out of a doorway down the hall. Her cornflower blonde curls were pinned up in a pretty updo, and she held in her arms a large ceramic bowl, in which she was mixing a wooden spoon rather furiously. "Oh, good. I was hoping she would get here between the storms. Welcome."

"This is my wife, Lily," Patrick said.

Lily was a stunning woman. She appeared to be all legs, and she had impeccable fashion sense. She even wore low kitten heels, black to match the hem of her red dress.

"Excuse my appearance." Lily smiled. "I was just finishing up the pound cake to throw in the oven."

"It's quite all right," I said.

"I hope you're hungry," Patrick said. "We're having a family favorite this evening. Bangers and mash."

My stomach growled. "That does sound good."

"Wonderful," Patrick said. "Here, why don't I show you to your room where you'll be staying first, and then we can have dinner?"

"All right," I said.

He led me up to a room on the second floor. It was a small space with a narrow bed. An adorable pink dollhouse stood in one corner, and stuffed toys filled the shelves along the wall. At the foot of the bed, a box overflowing with frilly dresses was only partially able to close, the colorful fabrics peeking out.

"I apologize for not having a proper space for you to stay in," Patrick said. "This is our daughter Amelia's room. She's agreed to share a room with her brother for the week."

"How kind of her," I said. "I know how difficult brothers can be."

Patrick grinned. "She'll appreciate hearing you say that. She's already complained about his toys all over the floor."

I smiled.

"Well, feel free to change if you wish. Otherwise, we will see you downstairs in a few moments. The washroom is at the end of the hall, the door on the right," Patrick said with a grin, starting to pull the door closed behind him.

"Patrick?" I said.

He stopped, leaning his head back into the room. "Yes?"

"Thank you," I said, hoping to convey the depth of my gratitude. "For allowing me to come and stay with you."

His smile warmed even further. "You are quite welcome, Helen. We are happy to have you."

He closed the door then, giving me a moment to collect myself.

I decided to change out of my dress, as it was still rather damp from the rain on the way to the station that morning. Freshening up in the washroom, I felt far more like myself...

Even if I was still having a hard time recognizing myself in the mirror.

I made my way downstairs a few moments later, and heard the happy cries of children.

A young girl ran past the stairs, shrieking with delight, her blonde pigtails bouncing as she hurried along. She darted into a doorway beside the bottom landing.

A little boy, perhaps only a year younger than she, charged after. He had the same dark hair as his father. "Ready or not," he cried. "I'm coming for you!"

His sister giggled as he followed after her into the room.

As I reached the bottom of the stairs, Patrick walked out of the doorway they had just passed through, a pair of oven mitts on and carrying a ceramic pan filled with steaming sausages. "All right now, be careful. The oven is very hot, and your mother is wielding a knife. We don't want her to accidentally add you both to the trifle."

"Da-a-ad," teased both of the children.

Patrick laughed, looking over at me. "Feeling refreshed?" he asked.

"I am, yes, thank you," I said. "Can I help with anything?"

"Not at all," he said. "You are our guest. Come along. The table's almost all set."

He walked down the hall, away from the stairs, and I followed after.

Taking a left, he walked into another room, and I found myself a moment later in a beautiful dining room.

Everything seemed to be antique, almost as if it had been taken right from a royal palace. The silverware was gleaming, and the dinnerware looked like the very best china. A candelabra stood in the center of the table, filled with dripping, flickering candles.

"This is such a beautiful room," I said.

Patrick laughed. "If you don't mind repeating that when Lily comes into the room, I would greatly appreciate it. She designed this room in an old fashioned style. She is quite the historical master."

"It's as if I stepped back in time," I said.

"That was the intent," Patrick said. "Now, we've set this place just for you." He gestured to the seat to the left of the head of the table. "Robert was the one who suggested you take his seat for the evening."

"Yeah," said a voice near the door. "I did.'

I turned and saw a little boy grinning up at me, a dark hole in place of his two front teeth.

"You must be Robert," I said. "You are very kind to let me have your seat. Thank you."

He beamed. "You are welcome, Miss."

Lily joined us a moment later, escorting little Amelia, who was still giggling furiously.

"Say hello to our guest, Amelia," Lily said, giving me an apologetic, amused smile.

Amelia climbed up into her chair, which was directly beside mine. "Hello, Miss. What's your name?"

"Helen," I said. "And you are Amelia."

She nodded firmly. "Yes. Do you like trifle? Because Mummy is making trifle for dessert."

"Oh, I love trifle," I said. "It's been such a long time since I've had it."

Amelia grinned. "Good. Mummy's trifle is the best trifle."

Lily plopped Robert down at the table, and took the seat directly across from me. Patrick then took the head of the table.

We said a prayer, and then Lily and Patrick both began to fill my plate with considerably more food than I would ever be able to eat.

"Please, you must be famished," Lily said. "Eat as much as you'd like."

"Oh, this is more than plenty," I said. "And it all looks wonderful."

It was. I hadn't eaten hardly anything all day. The potatoes were warm and buttery. The sausages were well seasoned, with a hint of spice. For as simple as it was, it was incredibly flavorful, and satisfying.

"Well, now, I must say...this dinner is well overdue," Patrick said with a smile as he sliced another sausage in half. "Every time you were in London seeing Roger, we were never able to make our schedules work. I am terribly sorry about that."

The food in my mouth suddenly tasted like ash, and it took a sip of cold water to force it down. We were going to start talking about Roger already...I supposed I should have expected as much.

"It's quite all right," I said. "Roger spoke of you often, Patrick. Meeting you both has made me wish we had met sooner as well."

"Oh, I do wish that Roger would have moved you to London," Lily said. "Though I understand why he didn't. It certainly is much safer out in the countryside. And none of us thought that the war would last as long as it has..."

"Wars are nothing more than a tool to make money," Patrick said. "And we who fight them are nothing more than pawns in their greed."

It was quite strange to speak so openly about Roger with people who actually had known him. Everyone in Brookminster only knew me, and what I spoke of him. And even though I had been married to him, Lily and Patrick were speaking about him as if they had known him better than I had.

With a pang of sorrow, I realized it was very likely the truth.

"But serving in the military isn't all bad," Patrick said, perhaps noticing the more somber expression on my face. "If there was no value in it, I would have left long ago."

"When did you join the military?" I asked.

"Oh, just out of school," he said. "That's where I met Roger, you know. We went to training together, and were stationed together in the same base for some time. When I turned twenty-five, I was moved into an office position, and he was taken away for some sort of further surveillance training. We lost touch for some time, but when both of our offices were brought together in London when the war broke out, we reconnected."

"I see," I said.

"He talked about you all the time, you know," Lily said. "Whenever he was here for dinner, he always commented on how you would have loved the décor, or the food, or the company. You were always on his mind."

My cheeks flushed pink, and I wasn't quite sure how to respond.

Lily's face fell, and she looked over at her husband with regret. "Oh, my heavens...how insensitive of me. I'm terribly sorry, Helen. Here I am, thinking that talking about Roger like this would be of comfort to you. I can clearly see how wrong I was about that."

"No, it's all right," I said, even though in my heart, I didn't believe the words that I said. If anything, I was starting to realize just how distant from Roger I really was.

I looked around the room, and my eyes fell on their children.

Roger and I likely would have had a child by now, had the war never broken out, I thought.

"I cannot imagine how difficult these last months have been for you, Helen," Lily said. "Six months has gone rather quickly, but I wonder if it's felt like a lifetime for you..."

My eyes stung, and I dearly wished that she would talk about something else. I wasn't sure how to voice that without being terribly rude, however.

"It certainly has," I said, trying to force a tight smile.

Lily reached out and laid her hand on top of her husband's, and they shared a touching, intimate sort of look, as if reading one another's thoughts.

It tugged on my heart, as I realized that Roger and I would never share a look like that ever again.

A stinging, poisonous sort of emotion began to seep through me, winding its way through my blood like a silent assassin.

Jealousy, I realized with a pang. *I'm...jealous of them. Jealous of what they have.*

Patrick sighed heavily, looking over at me, his hand still locked in his wife's. "Helen, I hope that you don't think we asked you to come stay with us just to make you feel bad," he said. "Because that is the very last thing we would want to do."

"Yes, of course," Lily said. "If you don't want us to talk about Roger any longer, than we certainly do not have to."

I met her gaze with my own questioning one.

No, it was not that I wished to stop talking about Roger... that was far from it.

"No," I said, shaking my head. "That's not it. Honestly, what I really want to know is what happened to him. What *really* happened to him."

Patrick set down his fork, which echoed around the quiet room with a distinct *clink*. He looked over at Lily, whose eyes were wide and troubled.

Patrick's jaw clenched, but he put on a smile in front of his children. "Well, I suppose I am not surprised. I was well aware that you were looking for more information in your letters..."

Lily got up from her seat, pushing it back as she rose. "Come along, Amelia, Robert..." she said, walking to Amelia's chair and pulling it back from the table. "You can finish eating in the kitchen."

"But why?" Robert asked, his little face screwing up with frustration. "I don't want to eat in the kitchen."

"Come along, dear," Lily said, more firmly, her gaze sharpening as she looked at her son.

Amelia's bottom lip was protruding. "But I want to eat with you and Daddy."

"I know, sweetheart," Patrick said. "But there is something very important that we must talk about with Mrs. Lightholder. Something that is only for grownups."

"I'm almost a grownup," Amelia said, sliding off her chair. "I'm almost seven."

"Yes, you are very grown up," Lily said, picking up both of their plates. "But this is a private conversation. You can come back in as soon as it's time for dessert."

She left the room, both children pouting at her heels.

Patrick looked apologetically over at me. "They are very good children," he said. "But just like all children, they dearly wish to be involved in everything the adults are doing."

"I do understand," I said. "And I certainly don't mean to trouble you and your family. That is the very last thing I wish to do, especially when you have been so hospitable, allowing me to stay with you."

Patrick smiled, and it eased the knots in my chest ever so slightly. "Now, now, we are very pleased to have you here with us," he said. "And I have had every intention of talking with you about all this. That is no imposition."

His face fell, and he looked away.

"Though I do wish that I could answer every question that I'm certain you will have – "

My heart lurched. He wished he could answer every question? "What do you mean by – "

"There now," Lily said, reappearing in the doorway, smoothing her skirt. "The children are all settled in the kitchen. Not very happily, mind you, but they'll be all right."

She resumed her seat at the table, a tight smile plastered on her face.

"What have I missed?" she asked, looking between Patrick and me.

Patrick cleared his throat. "Nothing much at all, dear. I was just telling Helen that I wish I were able to answer every question she will likely have, but – "

"I don't understand," I said, shaking my head. "In your

letters, you told me what happened to Roger. What caused his death."

Lily and Patrick exchanged another troubled looked.

"Yes, well...I am the one who likely knows the most about what happened to Roger, yes," Patrick said. "But even I am not privy to absolutely *everything*. Believe me, though... I've tried to find out as much as I could."

"Then...what can you tell me?" I asked, becoming more disheartened by the moment.

Patrick pushed his dinner plate aside, and leaned forward, his elbows resting on the table. "I hope that you are ready to hear all this, Helen," he said. "Because I am quite sure that Roger was not at all the man you thought he was."

3

R oger was not the man I thought he was?

That statement was shocking. Quite profound...and quite unbelievable.

"I might surprise you," I said. "I have spent a great many months pondering what happened to him, and I am certain there is nothing he could have done that was not something I have already considered."

Patrick nodded. "Perhaps you are right. And if that is the truth, then I hope this won't trouble you too greatly..."

Lily gave her husband an encouraging smile, squeezing his forearm affectionately.

"Roger Lightholder was not just a friend of mine. Yes, it's quite true what I told you just a few minutes ago. We did meet in the first weeks of our military careers. We were the best in our class, leagues better than any of the other men we were serving alongside. Our superiors saw potential in us, and quickly removed us from the others in order to train us specially."

Patrick paused thoughtfully.

"As I'm sure you know, your husband had a prestigious position, though there are very few who knew what that position was, precisely. Roger and I were separated some years later, where they trained me for an operatives position, and he was trained for something different." He gave me a very pointed look. "They wanted him for the intelligence department."

"Intelligence?" I asked, my brow furrowing.

He nodded, licking his lips. "When Roger and I were brought back together, we were told that I was to be his handler, or perhaps more accurately, his supervisor. And Roger...well, he was trained to be a spy, working with my department, which was, as I said, British intelligence."

It was as if I'd been struck. I wasn't sure if I had heard him correctly. I blinked once, twice...but Patrick still sat there, watching me carefully, the wrinkles on his forehead prominent in the candlelight.

"Maybe this is too much right now," Lily said, worry creasing her own brow, and she tugged gently on the sleeve of her husband's navy blue sweater. "Perhaps we should have some tea and the trifle, and give poor Helen a few moments to – "

"No," I said, feeling strangely lightheaded. "It's all right. I...it makes sense, in a way. I always knew his work was something dangerous. So dangerous that he didn't want me anywhere nearby, so as to keep me safe."

It was a great deal to comprehend. I knew it would take me some time before I was able to easily accept it.

Roger...a spy. How mindboggling.

"It killed him not to be able to tell you," Patrick said. "But his greatest concern was that if he did tell you, he would be putting you in danger. Any information that might drive his enemies toward you was never spoken of. He wanted to protect you in any possible way that he could."

It both tore me up, as well as warmed me to hear that about Roger. "I suppose I always knew that he was keeping things from me in order to protect me, and that it was a way that he showed how much he cared about me...but there is still a part of me that also wishes I could have known, so I could have helped him somehow – "

"There is no way you could have helped him," Patrick said. "I'm sorry, I don't mean to discourage you, but it's quite true. There was nothing you could have done for him. If anything, what might have been a temporary relief for him, telling you something, would have surely caused him many hours of stress and concern afterwards. I knew that part of Roger well, and his concern for you was primary."

I understood. It was hard to hear, but I did understand, deep down. It troubled me that I could not have comforted him, as his wife, but I had to realize that I hadn't just married a man. I married a man with a difficult position in life, and he had taken great risks by marrying me in the first place. I could see that now.

"Is there anything else you can tell me?" I asked, hopeful.

He pursed his lips, exhaling through his nose. "Well...to be honest, there isn't a great deal I can say, no. I'm already putting you at great risk by telling you all this in the first place. Are you certain you would want to know more?"

"Of course," I said. "There is still so much I don't know. Yes, he was a – a spy," I said, tripping over my words slightly. That was going to take some getting used to saying...if I ever spoke of it again outside this room. "But that doesn't explain his death, or why it happened. Not fully."

Patrick nodded slowly. "Very well," he said. "I will tell you, but just for the sake of my friendship with the man... and because he loved you so very dearly."

I smiled gratefully at him.

"In the months leading up to...well, everything that went on, Roger was beginning to unearth information about our enemies that was deeply troubling," he said, worry drawing the wrinkles in his face out even more. I noticed a scar just underneath his eye gleaming in the dim light from the candles. "I was under the impression that our enemies had been working diligently to infiltrate our networks, leeching information from lower soldiers, disguising themselves, hiding among us...and Roger learned that was, in fact, correct. At least, most of it."

A chill ran down my spine. While I had been safe and secure back in Plymouth, wondering when I might be able to see my husband again, he was here in London, sniffing out enemy infiltration.

We had lived such different lives, utterly disconnected from one another.

"With very little help from anyone else, Roger managed to discover an undercover German operative who had made his way into the chain of command above me. Roger came to me late one night, his face as pale as a ghost, sweating profusely...and when I asked him what was causing him so much distress, he quickly shut my door, and dragged me into the closet in my office."

Patrick rubbed the back of his neck, his gaze distant as he reflected on the events he described.

"He told me in a hurried whisper that he'd located the spy, someone I'd never met before, who was using some sort of alias, and that he was working in Klein's office. Klein was the man I reported to, and this German spy had somehow wormed his way into his confidence. At first, it was incredibly hard to believe. Klein was a decorated soldier himself. He could tell if a man was lying just by looking at him. So I questioned Roger, finding it incredibly hard to believe what he was telling me. Roger insisted, and after revealing this, he fled my office..."

Patrick shook his head, rubbing his temples with his fingertips.

"If I had known what was to come next, I never would have let him leave without me, or at least without another soldier to keep watch on him..." Patrick said, clearly straining to get the words out.

"Patrick, sweetheart..." Lily murmured.

Patrick shook his head. "It's all right, my love. Helen needs to hear this."

He straightened, cleared his throat, and pressed on.

"The next three days passed, and I heard nothing from Roger. I was beginning to worry, when I was called into Klein's office, just before leaving for the day. It was February 18th. It was snowing. It was bitter and cold. Klein told me that our office had been compromised, and that we were all going to be moved to new places of employment throughout the city. He gave me a list of names that I was meant to give the newest instructions to, and I realized quickly that Roger's name was not on the list. When I challenged him on it, Klein told me quite plainly...'*There was an air raid in London last night. Late at night. We lost some good men.*' I looked at him blankly, and protested. The last bombing had been weeks before, and we had done what we could to keep that in confidence, as well. No one had perished in that raid, but there certainly was no bombing the night before. Klein's eyes were blazing, and he said simply, *'Roger died in the bombings that occurred last night.'* I challenged him once again, but he cut me off. *'Yes, he did'* he said, deathly serious."

Patrick licked his lips, his eyes attempting to bore a hole into the table.

"That was meant to be the story, but from what Klein alluded to, Roger's discovery was found out by the spy...and it was in fact the spy that killed him...not any air raid."

I sat back in the seat, his words ringing in my ears.

Something in me had suspected that the stories I'd been told were not true. There had been reports of air raids in London more than once during the war, but when I received the phone call telling me that Roger had been killed in one...something had felt...wrong.

"But the newspaper," I said. "It confirmed what I'd been told by the soldier that called me. There had been bombings, and some soldiers had perished."

Patrick shook his head. "Entirely invented. Even the names of the other soldiers were false."

My head was starting to feel as if it were being stuffed full, and threatened to pop. The blood pounded in my skull, and a dull ache began behind my eyes. "But why?" I asked. "Why lie about it to everyone?"

"Klein and others were unwilling to allow the enemy spy to know that we'd become aware of the weak link on our security, or of his infiltration. It was feared that the truth would send him into hiding, which it most certainly would have. They decided it was best to permanently obscure the details about Roger's death. As far as anyone outside this room knows, Roger was killed in the bombings."

"We are the only ones who know?" I breathed.

Patrick nodded. "Us and about three others, Klein included."

"And what happened to the spy?" I asked.

Patrick exhaled, looking away. "That's where this all gets trickier. After I was informed about the truth, I was excluded from any further investigations. I have been forbidden from asking about it, as it is now being handled internally. Unfortunately, you and I will likely never get the full truth about what has transpired since then."

"We don't even know if they caught the spy?" I asked.

Patrick shook his head. "No, but I would be terribly surprised if they haven't. They were very discreet about his death, and about revealing it. And if they haven't found him, they will soon enough."

"What if he kills again?" I asked. "What will they do then?"

"Helen, I know this is deeply troubling. Trust me, there have been many nights where I've lain awake, wondering if this spy might ever learn of my connection to Roger and decide to come after me in revenge. But Roger's whole job was to infiltrate the Germans, and learn the truth about them. That was why he was so worried about protecting you from any and all information. If they learned that you knew anything, they surely would have come after you."

"I had wondered about that myself..." I mumbled.

Patrick nodded. "I understand how this must be incredibly discouraging to you. But at least you know the truth now. Your husband died a hero, trying to do what he could to keep our country safe. As much as I dislike saying it, his death was as honorable as if he had been killed in battle."

"I suppose you're right," I said.

Lily suddenly came to life once again, reaching across

the table to pick up my empty glass. "All right, we have the whole week to discuss these things. Patrick, I think poor Helen needs some time to think through all you have told her. It's quite a lot to digest."

Patrick looked over at me, his mouth slightly open. "Yes, I suppose so," he said. "Why don't we have a break?" I don't want your entire trip here to be so morose."

My heart heavy, I tried to smile anyways. "Yes, I agree."

"Good," Lily said, clearly relieved. She stood up from the table. "I'll go finish up the trifle, and we can all go back to having a pleasant evening, all right?"

"Very well, darling," Patrick said.

Lily nodded and hurried from the room.

"These things make Lily jumpy," Patrick said. "Roger has been a frequent topic of discussion here at our home. I've had many colleagues come to visit, wondering what really happened to him. They, like you, were not fooled by the articles in the paper...even if their superiors swore by the accuracy of the statement. They just couldn't believe that a soldier like Roger would have been taken out that way. The bombing excuse took the blame entirely off of Roger, though...and so I've stood by it, lying over and over again to those who have come to me with – well, hello there, Robert. Come in, come in."

Little footsteps echoed in the hall, and a small, wide-eyed face appeared in the doorway of the dining room.

The conversation was at its end, and part of me was relieved.

"Here we are," Lily said, leading Amelia back into the room, the trifle in a lovely glass bowl, tucked beneath her other arm. "Now, who's hungry?"

4

I found myself at the Gordon's residence the next morning all alone.

Lily had made a delicious, hearty breakfast, which Patrick consumed rather hastily before hurrying out the door in his military best. He kissed Lily, Amelia, and Robert all on the cheek, and gave me a warm smile as he picked up his briefcase from beside the front door.

"Now, I need to take the children off to school," Lily said. "You are free to stay here and rest, if you'd like. Or go and explore the city. Whatever you choose, I will leave you the key, and I will just see you when I get back."

London held no attraction for me, and so I chose to while away the morning in the comfort of their home. I stayed in Amelia's room, mostly, reading through some of the books I'd brought with me for entertainment.

It didn't take me long, however, to realize that I was just not going to be able to concentrate. Not after everything I'd learned the night before.

I wandered downstairs, very aware of my footsteps

echoing on the polished wooden floors. I felt strange, exploring their house, even the more public spaces, when Lily and Patrick were not home.

Even still, I found a handsome study that doubled as a library. There was also a pleasant conservatory at the back of the house, overlooking the small, fenced garden where toys lay scattered in the grass, left over from some grand adventure of the imagination.

I eventually found myself back in the sitting room near the front door, uncomfortable with sitting anywhere else.

But that was all I wanted to do. Sit, and think.

I wasn't sure how to process everything Patrick had said. There was a small part of me, far deep down, that railed against what he had revealed. *No, it can't be true. Roger wasn't a spy. Why would a spy have gotten married? Wouldn't he have known that his death was likely? Why would he have put me through that?*

But what reason would Patrick Gordon have to lie to me? I could think of nothing.

On top of that, I'd never known what Roger's work truly was. And if it hadn't been something as secretive or important as a spy, then why wouldn't he have told me? Officers' and generals' wives knew what their husbands did, or at least knew a great deal more than I did about Roger.

It made sense...I just was having a hard time believing it.

It was half past one when the front door opened, and Lily's voice echoed down the front hall. "Hello? Helen? Are you here?"

I rose from my spot in the sitting room. "Yes, here I am," I said.

Lily appeared in the doorway, wearing an adorable hat with a felt flower attached to it. It looked homemade, given the jagged edge of some of the petals. She smiled at me as she pulled the hat off. "Have you had a pleasant morning?"

"As pleasant as one in my position could have, I suppose," I said, walking toward the doorway. I smiled at her. "I appreciate you opening your home to me. And allowing me to speak with your husband last night."

Lily's face softened even further, and she smiled, her bright red painted lips stretching across her pretty face. "It is the very least we can do. As hard as it was to hear, I'm sure you are quite relieved to know the truth," she said as she turned and started toward the kitchen, setting her hat atop a peg on the wall as she passed.

I followed after her. "Well, I thought I would too...but instead, I'm having a hard time comprehending it all."

Lily stood at the sink, filling a tea kettle with water. "I thought you might. Giving you a night to sleep on it was best, but trust me...I can understand perfectly how difficult it is to accept what it is that our husband's do...and to also accept that there is a great deal we will never know about it all."

She sat down at the small, round kitchen table, moving aside coloring pages and a box of crayons that Amelia had been hard at work on that morning at breakfast.

I took the seat at the table across from her. "But it seems as if you know so much."

Lily shook her head. "No. I don't, honestly. Even being married for twelve years now, I don't know what Patrick's day to day looks like. I've met some of the men he answers to, like General Klein, for example. But when people ask me what it is that my husband does, I simply tell them he is a commander in the military. Everyone is always very impressed, of course, as I'm sure you can relate."

"Yes, I can relate," I said. "And there were always those who wanted to pry, asking too many questions. It always made me uncomfortable."

"I know what that's like," Lily said. "There are always those who are too nosy for their own good."

The tea kettle on the stove began to whistle, and she rose quickly to tend to it. "Would you care for some tea?" she asked, glancing over her shoulder. "I always feel as if tea is a balm for the weary soul."

I smiled. "Yes, I would very much like some. Thank you."

She poured us some fresh, hot tea, and returned to the table, setting my cup down before me. "There we are..." she said, resuming her seat across from me.

I sipped at the hot beverage, nearly scalding my tongue. It was comforting, however. I couldn't be bothered to slow down as I chanced another sip.

"I admire your bravery, you know," Lily said. "I cannot even imagine what it must have been like for you...losing Roger. I know I would just be beside myself – " she stopped suddenly, her eyes widening. "I'm sorry. I keep saying those sorts of insensitive things, don't I?"

"It's all right," I said. "It was hard. Incredibly so. To be honest, I found myself angry at Roger a lot of the time. I wanted to know why he had to be in London like he was, when he was. I was angry that I couldn't have been with him when he died...or at least nearby. I hadn't seen him in weeks leading up to his death, and it's clear that I had absolutely no idea what was going on in his life. He probably hardly thought of me before he died."

Now it was my turn to be embarrassed. My cheeks flooded with color, and I moaned in regret.

"How selfish am I?" I said, covering my face with my

hands. "Roger was trying to save the country, trying to do his part for the war...and all I can think about is myself?"

"It's all right," Lily said, reaching across the table. "You don't have to feel bad about that. You loved him, and it's clear you still do. It's only natural to wonder these things."

I frowned, shaking my head. "How could he do this to me?" I asked. "I keep wondering...why did he even ask me to marry him if he knew something this terrible could happen?"

Lily surprised me by smiling. "I thought that much would have been obvious," she said. "He was madly in love with you. I knew he was going to propose to you the moment he showed up at our house and told us that he'd met someone."

She leaned forward, her smile widening.

"Where did you two meet, anyway? He told Patrick, but I only ever heard half the story."

The memories came flooding back, filling my mind. "Well...we met at the park, actually. It was early June, and I was visiting a friend here in London. Roger was playing cricket with some friends, and one of their plays landed the ball right beside our picnic blanket. Roger came running over to collect it, and when we saw each other..." I paused, the color in my face deepening.

"That's wonderful," Lily said. "A proper love story. Then what happened?"

"Well, according to his friends, he ruined their whole game because all he wanted to do was sit there with us and talk. We offered him a sandwich, which he happily accepted. We exchanged names, and my friend gave him her number in case he wanted to call, which rather caught me off guard."

"Did he?" Lily asked. "Call, I mean?"

I smiled, in spite of myself. "Yes, he did. That very night, in fact. And my friend wouldn't let me say no, even though we had plans to go to the theater to see a play. She insisted that I take him instead. And...well, that was really the start of it all, I suppose."

Lily beamed at me. "How exciting. That explains why he was so utterly giddy when he came by for dinner a few weeks later. I've never seen a man so in love before."

It was as if a stone had been tied around my heart, and someone had tossed it into the depths of the sea.

"Oh, dear, what's the matter?" Lily asked, her brow furrowing. "Did I say something – "

I shook my head, my eyes welling with tears. I could do nothing to stop them. "No," I said, my face starting to burn. "No, I just...I wish I could have had closure. Even though I know the truth now, I still have so many questions."

"There, there..." Lily said, patting my arm affectionately. "It's quite all right. And I understand. But there is something you must understand. There will likely be questions that you will never have answered. I know that's true for my marriage, and it took me a long time to accept it."

I dabbed at my eyes with the corner of a napkin that Lily offered me. "But how?" I asked. "It feel as if it's eating me from the inside."

She nodded. "It certainly does. I wrestled with the same thoughts for years. It caused me so much grief...far too much, if I'm honest."

"How did you come to terms with it?" I asked.

"You just have to," she said. "I had to learn to make peace with it. For myself. For my own mind. I knew that if I were to continue to live that way, I would be robbing myself of life's greatest joys. My husband. My children. Our friends. Our community. And I suppose one day...I just realized that wasn't the way I wanted to live."

I took a long, slow sip of my tea once again, thinking.

Since Roger died...I have had no peace. Not any. It doesn't matter that I've tried. Peace has done nothing but elude me.

"I understand what that's like," I said. "That's how I feel right now. I even...I even moved away from home to an entirely new place, completely on a whim, with the hope that I might be able to put my past behind me."

Lily shook her head. "It doesn't work like that. We can never run from our pasts. They always find a way to follow after us, reminding us that they are still there."

"I had desperately hoped that Brookminster would be the place where I could start over, begin my life anew..."

"And there is nothing wrong with that," Lily said. "But a place is not going to replace your husband, or help you to forget about him. You likely never will. You will just learn to deal with the pain in your own way."

"It makes me wonder if I was too hasty in my decision to move," I said. "Perhaps I would have been better off had I decided to stay in Plymouth with my family and friends..."

"You may never know," Lily said. "But the answer may not be to completely uproot yourself again and move back to be sure."

I looked up at her, smiling halfheartedly. "You are quite perceptive, Lily. How did you know I was thinking just that?"

"Because it is precisely what I would have thought to do as well," she said. "But you have been there for how long now...four months? Five?"

"Just about, yes," I said. "I moved in March."

"Then you must have some new friends, some sort of life

that you are enjoying. I mean, if you hadn't, then surely you would have left by now?" Lily asked.

I considered her words, and realized quickly how right she was.

"Indeed," I said. "I do have new friends. And I think it would hurt them if I were to leave. Some were even wondering if I was considering it, when I was preparing to come here for the week."

"And how would you feel if you left them?" she asked.

I thought of Irene, her husband, and their son. They were practically family to me now. They always cared for me so much, and went far out of their way to help me.

I thought of Sidney, my neighbor, also new to Brookminster. He had been a wonderful friend, going above and beyond, helping me with anything that I ever needed help with. Not only was he handy, but he was wonderful company. He always seemed to know exactly what to say to make me laugh.

I thought about Inspector Graves, and the unlikely friendship that had developed between us. He had been reluctant to allow me to help with all of the latest troubles in Brookminster, but had come around. The truth was, we made a good team, working off each other very well. He was strong where I was weak, and vice versa.

"You're right..." I said, smiling at her, wiping the last of the tears from my eyes. "I suppose that it would be foolish to be so impulsive, and pick up and leave. Especially now."

"Good," Lily said, smiling. "That is where healing begins, after all. And perhaps now you can find that peace you are looking for...knowing the truth like you do."

"Perhaps I can," I said. "I certainly hope so."

5

The rest of the week with the Gordons passed in a comfortable blur. They were so utterly kind to me, and it felt as if I had known them for years. Their affection for Roger had translated very easily to me, and I felt like I could have gotten along with them quite well had Roger still been alive, and was rather regretful when the last night of my stay came upon us.

"Do you really have to leave?" Amelia asked me as she sat upon my lap, a book clutched in her hands, pouting up at me.

"I do," I said. "I have a shop that I need to go back to."

"The haba-dash-..." she started. "The haberdasher...y?"

I laughed. "Yes. There will be many ladies in my village who will be looking for replacements for their buttons for their coats, and zippers for their skirts, and buckles for their shoes. And if I know little Brookminster at all, I will have quite a few dashing men at my door, inquiring after my silk for handkerchiefs and ties."

"We have really enjoyed having you here, Helen," Patrick

said from the floor where he played with wooden blocks with Robert. "I hope you know that you are welcome at any time."

"Yes, you certainly are," Lily said. "We would love to have you over once again. Perhaps in autumn. We could take you to the market, and show you around some of Roger's favorite places."

I smiled. "I would like that."

The next morning, I was waving goodbye to Lily and the children; Patrick had already left for work. I stood beside the cab, my heart aching. It felt as if I was saying goodbye to Roger...or at least those who helped me to feel the closest tie with his memories.

"Please make sure to call when you arrive back at home," Lily said. "Have a safe trip!"

Amelia's bottom lip was protruding, and she soon burst into tears, burying her face in her mother's skirt.

"Take care," I said. "Thank you again!"

I climbed into the cab, the echo of the smile still on my face.

The cab driver, a rail of a man with bad teeth, turned around and grinned. "It's always hard to leave family, isn't it?"

I smiled. "Yes, I suppose it is."

I told him which station I was leaving from. Patrick had kindly found a better price, and time, for a train, and had booked it for me. He wouldn't accept any form of payment to cover it, either.

I arrived at the station when the sun was shining high above us, and it was quite warm. I was all too pleased to get inside the station, despite all of the people who seemed to be taking the same train I was.

Elbow to elbow I pushed my luggage trolley toward the platform, but my mind was on the week I'd spent with Patrick, Lily, and their children.

It was a very pleasant week. I learned a great many things about Roger that I had never known. I learned that his favorite treat was an ice lolly, particularly the cherry flavored kind. I learned that he spent mornings strolling down by the Thames, reading letters that I'd written to him. I learned that his favorite songs were from Mozart, and that he played piano when he was a boy.

I learned some of his favorite meals from Lily, things that he'd hoped we could one day make together. Patrick told me that he was quite good at playing card games, often winning all the money off the other soldiers when there were quiet nights on duty. Amelia and Robert told me that he would ride around in the living room on hands and knees, neighing like a pony so that Robert would tire himself out enough to go to sleep at night.

It was as if I was falling in love with him all over again... and it broke my heart.

I had asked Patrick for more information about Roger's death, but he was unable to give me any. "I told you everything I can," he said with a shrug. "I would tell you more if I knew anything. I promise to let you know if I find anything else out, though. I promise."

I believed him when he said that.

The trip back home to Brookminster seemed to take longer than it had the first time. I couldn't get comfortable on the train, no matter how I sat. The old man who was sitting in the cabin beside me was snoring, his mouth hanging open, spittle trailing down his chin. A young infant cried mercilessly, her mother trying desperately to comfort her by walking up and down the length of the car.

It didn't matter, though. I was going home, and I knew that I couldn't wait to arrive.

I stared out the window as the countryside rolled past, my mind racing as I enjoyed the sight of the hills and the sheep farms as the train raced by.

Even though Lily had warned me there was a chance I would never get all the answers I was looking for, I had at least learned the truth about Roger's death. And that was more than I thought might happen.

But even still...there remained a great deal that Patrick Gordon didn't know, information that Roger must have discovered before his death. Roger may have learned who the mole was that had infiltrated their ranks, but apart from that, he had revealed very little. Was it possible that the information he'd discovered was still out there somewhere, in some form that could be discovered in the future?

Well, there were likely very few people Roger could trust with that sort of information, especially if he wasn't completely certain who this spy was. How long was he searching, afraid of those he worked with? Did he suspect it all along?

It was frustrating, not being able to know. These questions had chased themselves around in my mind all week. I finally had the courage to voice them to Patrick on the last night, and what he said had rather surprised me.

"Well, it's possible that he hid his notes somewhere, though he never would have left them in plain black and white," he said.

"Plain black and white? What do you mean by that?" I'd asked.

"We would never find a notebook where he'd written something like *I'm suspicious of Sergeant Green,* or anything like that. If he wanted to leave clues behind, he likely would have left them in the form of a cypher. A code of some sort. Spies use them often in order to communicate secret messages that can go without detection by the ordinary eye. I thought the same thing after his death, but I've gone through every letter he wrote to me within six months of his death, and found nothing."

That got me thinking, though, that perhaps he hadn't sent letters written with those cyphers to Patrick at all.

...What if he'd sent them to me, instead?

I realized it was quite a stretch, thinking Roger's letters would have been anything aside from just that. Letters. Especially given his desire to protect me from anything that had any connection to him whatsoever. Wouldn't he have realized that someone might try to come after me if they suspected he had been sending me secret information?

It isn't entirely impossible to think that he might have buried some vital information in his letters to me, I thought, the train rumbling along toward a dark patch of clouds in the distance. *What if he did, and hoped that I would read between the lines, realizing there was invisible information imbedded within?*

It did seem a bit farfetched, and yet...

If there is, somehow, this information buried within my letters, then surely he would have wanted me to pass that information on.

A sobering thought struck me.

...Did he know that he was going to die? In the weeks leading to his death, he was sending me more letters than he usually did... and they were quite a bit longer than normal, as well.

This was intriguing.

My enthusiasm was quickly extinguished, though.

This may seem like a good idea, but it's impossible for me to examine the letters he sent me any closer...seeing as how they were all stolen when that thief broke into my home.

As the train began to slow, coming close to the station just inside of Gloucestershire, I was beginning to put some more of the pieces together of the mysteries surrounding me.

Roger must have embedded some sort of code into my letters. Why else would the thief have stolen them?

I was very nearly positive that was the reason as I gathered my suitcase from the luggage rack and walked off the train.

I hoped that I would have the chance to speak with Sam Graves about the matter. He'd promised me that in my absence he would look further into the break ins that had happened in my home. I was well aware that Sam had no success in finding any clues before I'd left, and so there was little cause to suspect he would have found much while I was gone.

Still...I feared those letters were now in the wrong hands. What if I had somehow unknowingly allowed this all to occur, and betrayed Roger's trust, albeit unintentionally? If he had left any sort of message, what if the plans that he and the others had laid in place were now in jeopardy?

I had to find those letters. And who stole them.

On top of all that, I was starting to think...no, believe now...that the person who had been stalking me in the shadows of the alleyway was the same person who'd broken into my house. They'd likely been watching my every move, awaiting a time when I wasn't home to strike. How many of my conversations had this person overheard? Was it someone hiding in plain sight, someone I knew? Or was it someone who was just always off to the side, just out of my view, yet all the while knowing precisely who I was and what information I likely possessed?

Either way, it was troubling...and made me all the more concerned about returning home to Brookminster.

I must get to the bottom of all this, I thought as I walked away from the much quieter, much smaller platform. *I will not let Roger down.*

I moved my trolley out into the foyer of the station, the dark clouds rumbling overhead.

*What a joy to return home just before a storm...*I thought darkly.

George, Irene's brother, was waiting for me at the station in his cab. I'd called Irene the night before to let her know my change in plans, and she'd promised to let her brother know. Apparently, he'd received the message.

"Welcome back," he said brightly as I approached, eyeing the clouds overhead warily, just waiting for them to open up upon us. "It's good to see you. How was your trip?"

"It was very pleasant, thank you," I said.

He scooped up my suitcase as easily as if it weighed no more than a book, and walked it back to the boot. "That's good to hear. And your family's doing well?"

"Oh, they're not my – " I said, but then caught myself. They very well may as well have been my family, given Patrick's relationship with Roger. "Well, they aren't *my* family. They're my late husband's, but I suppose that's all semantics, anyway."

George laughed. "I know what you mean. My ex-wife's family was *her* family, and I was happy to keep it that way."

"Well, it wasn't like that," I said as we both climbed into

the cab. "I just had never met them before, but now I suppose I would be happy to count them among my family as well."

"That's good to hear," George said. "You know, Irene was missing you something awful. Michael, too. He said on Friday last that he wished you were there to eat some of his mother's rhubarb pie with him."

I smiled. "Yes, they've started having me over on Friday evenings. It was rather strange not being there with them this week."

George gave me a wry, sidelong look. "I'm starting to think you spend more time with my nephew than I do."

"Oh, no, I wouldn't say that," I said, my cheeks flooding with color. "I just happen to find myself at the tea house often throughout the week. They've certainly established one of the coziest places in the village, haven't they?"

"Indeed they have," George said, in all of his good humor. "I was just teasing, you know. My family knows I love them. But I'm glad that you've knit yourself to Irene. She needed someone like you."

"I needed her, too," I said, smiling.

He asked me about my trip, and I freely told him about all the excitement of London, and all the wonderful food that Lily had made for me. I was discreet with the Gordons' names, not wanting to bring any sort of undue attention to them, either.

George then told me about all the car trouble he had been having while I was gone, and how grateful he was to be able to have a car that was functioning properly. He said it took him, Sidney Mason, and another man in the village nearly three days to distinguish the problem.

"That Sidney, though. He's a hard worker, isn't he? Won't

take no for an answer, either. He said he was going to figure out what the problem was, and by Jove, he sure did."

"He is quite persistent, yes," I said with a small laugh. "But very handy."

"Yes he certainly is," George said. "I swear, that man knows something about everything, doesn't he? Carpentry, electrical, plumbing, mechanical...it doesn't matter what it is. If he can tinker with it, he can figure it out."

"A bit crazy, if you ask me," I said, and George and I shared a laugh together.

We arrived in Brookminster a short time later, and he dropped me off at home. "Glad you had a nice trip," he said with a big smile. "But I'm sure it's nice to be home again."

I looked up at the honey-colored cottage, the ivy curling up the northern walls, the shutters all thrown open to let the warm summer light in whenever it decided to make an appearance. It certainly was home.

"Yes," I said, feeling more relieved upon my return than when I'd left. "It is nice to be back."

I said goodbye to George, who got back into his car after depositing my suitcase in the house for me, and drove off back into town.

I dragged my suitcase back up the stairs, and decided it was best to spend my time unpacking, as opposed to allowing my clothes to stay folded up inside, just waiting for me to get them nice and clean once again.

Setting a kettle on the burner, I went about getting my home in order. I noticed Irene had left a small package of leftovers in my ice box, ready for me to enjoy for dinner that evening.

I smiled. Irene, ever thoughtful.

I was pouring some tea into a mug for myself when I heard a knock somewhere downstairs.

Pausing, I turned my ear toward the door leading downstairs.

The knock came again.

I rolled my eyes, tension gripping the muscles in my back. *I just returned home. If this is a customer, then I sincerely hope they have a very good reason for –*

But it wasn't a customer. It was Sidney Mason's smiling face in the window beside my back door. He was holding onto the straps of a bag, which hung over his shoulder.

I unlocked the door and pulled it open. "Sidney, hello," I said.

He grinned. "I saw your lights on, figured you must've gotten home. I'm not interrupting, am I?"

"Oh, no, it's quite all right," I said, stepping aside. "Would you care for some tea? I just made a fresh kettle."

"That sounds wonderful," he said. "It'll give me a chance to get out of this rain that's coming."

We walked up to my flat, hearing the thunder roll outside, making the glass in the windows tremble.

"My goodness, I think we are in for quite the storm," Sidney said, smiling as we reached the landing in the kitchen.

More thunder growled, like a hunting lion, up above.

"I think you are right," I said. I walked over to the kettle, retrieved a second cup from my cupboard, and began to pour some tea for him.

"When did you arrive home?" he asked.

"Oh, not even an hour ago," I said, bringing our tea over to the table before turning to fetch the sugar. "I'm afraid I don't have any cream."

"That's quite all right," he said. "I can drink it black. Not a problem."

I took the seat across from him, my heart caught in my throat.

He really was a handsome man. His eyes were so clear, and the golden hues in his ginger hair revealed his recent days out in the sunshine. His beard had grown in somewhat since I'd left.

I loved the way his freckles spread across his face when he smiled, which he was doing now. "I hope I am not bothering you, coming over as soon as you were home. I thought perhaps you had returned yesterday and I just hadn't seen you."

"No, today," I said.

He smiled. "It's good to see you, you know. A week seemed like a great deal of time."

My heart warmed at his words. "It's good to see you, too, Sidney," I said.

"How was your trip?" he asked, bringing his tea to his lips. "Did you manage to find any of the answers you were looking for?"

I opened my mouth to talk about the fascinating trip I'd had...when something at the back of my mind made me catch myself. I remembered Patrick's words, urging me to keep the things I'd learned secret, reminding me that I was one of the very few people privy to the information I now knew.

I liked Sidney. I really did. But that didn't mean I needed to share every piece of information that I'd learned with him. He was not very forthcoming with information about his own life, after all. There was no reason to have to reveal anything that I'd discovered.

I smiled, looking down into my teacup. "It was absolutely wonderful to see a friend of Roger's, and to share some good memories about him. It was cathartic. There were some emotional moments, especially when we all talked about his death, and what our lives had been without him since..." I said. "To be honest, I feel much more at peace with everything. I think it's precisely the trip I needed."

Sidney nodded, but his gaze was striking as he searched my face. He remained quiet, as if expecting me to carry on.

I took a cautious sip of my tea, checking to make sure it wasn't too hot, but also to avoid having to say any more.

For a moment I could have sworn I saw his eyes narrowing. The expression passed quickly, though, and he smiled again. "Well, I'm glad to hear it. Really. Oh, before I forget..."

He reached down to the pack he'd set down at his feet, unzipped it, and procured a small package wrapped in brown paper.

"It's nothing much, just a bit of bread I made this afternoon," he said. "I made too much, so I thought I'd bring some over and see if you were home."

I took the package. The bread was still warm within.

I smiled at him. "Thank you, Sidney. It really is good to be home."

He smiled back at me. "It's good to have you back, and I know I speak for everyone when I say that."

6

The next morning was Monday, which I was grateful for, as I had planned on having the shop closed for one more day. I had everything all planned for a relaxing time for myself. I wanted to rearrange some of my clothes, and work on a new project I had been inspired to work on when I had seen one of Lily's dresses.

I wanted to enjoy a hot, luxurious bath, and read a book out in my back garden...as long as Sidney was out working that day and not at home, otherwise I knew I would spend all afternoon talking with him.

It had been pleasant seeing him the night before. I thought it sweet, even, that he had noticed my lights on and decided to come and see me. Not to mention the bread he'd brought to me was absolutely delicious.

He said that nothing exciting had happened to my house during the week, and he had kept a very close eye on it. I knew he certainly would have, and it was a relief to know that nothing else had happened in my absence. It wasn't as if my mysterious burglar could have stolen much more. If they were after the letters, they had found what they wanted.

Something told me that the thief wouldn't be back to bother me anytime soon.

I was just about to sit down in my back room with my sewing machine when the telephone rang.

I made my way out to the kitchen, wondering who it could be. Did anyone even know I was home yet?

"Hello?" I said, picking the phone up off the receiver.

"Helen?" said the voice. "It's Sam Graves calling."

My eyes widened. "Sam? Well, hello."

"Hello," he repeated, then cleared his throat. A phone rang somewhere in the background, and I heard someone yelling at someone else. "I, um...I wasn't sure if you were home from your trip or not. I thought I remembered you saying that you came in on Sunday evening."

"I did," I said. "Arrived home yesterday afternoon."

"Very good," he said.

There was a pause on the other end, and I would have thought the call had been cut off had it not been for the sound of someone typing on a typewriter, or the cackling laughter of some woman.

"Well, I was calling to see if you were busy this afternoon," he said. "Have you reopened your shop yet?"

"No, not yet," I said, my brow creasing. "I was giving myself a day to get settled back into life here."

He said, "Well, I certainly wouldn't want to bother you if you had other plans, but I was wondering if you might be available for lunch."

I blinked, my eyes unfocused on the room around me. Did he...ask me out to lunch? "For what?" I asked, suddenly nervous. "Is everything all right?"

"Oh, yes of course, everything is perfectly fine," he said. "I was – well, I simply wanted to – I suppose I was just wondering how your trip back to London was, and if you were able to find out anything that you had been searching for."

"Oh," I said. I glanced over at the clock. "Well, I suppose I could meet you for lunch. What time, and where should we meet?"

Sam cleared his throat. "How about in an hour? At the inn?"

"I can do that," I said.

"Wonderful," Sam said. "I'll see you there soon."

As I hung up, I felt confused. *That was a rather formal invitation...wasn't it? It certainly didn't feel like how he would normally ask me to do things with him...*

I brushed my hair from my eyes, trying to collect my thoughts.

As I made my way back toward my room, and more aptly, toward my closet, I stopped dead in my tracks.

Was this...was this a romantic outing?

Did I just agree to step out with Sam Graves?

That was quite a revelation. And quite the turn of events.

But that couldn't be right...could it?

I thought back to the night when we had been driving to go and speak with Evangeline, the daughter of Abigail Lowell who had been killed some weeks before. He had made some mention about how I wouldn't have been a bad dinner companion, and had been rather sheepish about it.

During our phone call, as well, he seemed nervous.

Sam Graves? Nervous? It seemed like an oxymoron.

Or was it possible that I was misunderstanding his intentions entirely?

That was likely the truth. This couldn't be a romantic engagement. It was probably something more business related, knowing Sam.

I got ready as I usually would, but found I spent a little bit of extra time on my hair, trying a hairstyle that I had seen Lily wear that I rather liked. I used a new lipstick that I'd been saving for a special occasion. I wore a dress in an emerald green that brought out the blue in my eyes.

There's nothing wrong with me wanting to look nice, I thought as I held up earrings against my dress to find the pair that looked the best. *This isn't anything romantic. I wouldn't have wanted it to be romantic in the first place.*

...Or would I?

If I was honest, I wasn't sure which I wanted it to be.

I decided it was best not to agonize over it until I knew for sure. I needed to see how he would react to me.

I headed out to the inn a short time later, more nervous than I had expected to be. I tried to gather my emotions as I walked down High Street, the Honey and Rose coming into view. It was as charming as ever, perhaps even more so given the sunlight glinting off the windows, and all the beautiful pink geraniums growing in the flower boxes beneath the windows of the upper story.

I pushed the front door open, and stepped inside the inn.

Heavenly scents of rosemary and sage reached me as soon as I walked over the threshold. I wasn't sure if it was bread, or some sort of roasted meat, or perhaps even some sort of vegetable, but regardless, it smelled so good that it made my mouth water.

"Helen Lightholder."

I turned and saw Sam rising from a chair beside the

door. He adjusted his jacket, which was not at all the one I usually saw him wearing at the police station.

"Good afternoon, Inspector Graves," I said.

He walked up to me, his piercing blue eyes gluing me to the spot, as if freezing me in place. "I trust you are well?"

"I am, yes," I said, surprised once again by his formality. "And yourself?"

"I am well," he said. "Shall we go to our table?"

"Yes," I said.

He turned rather rigidly, and headed toward the dining room.

My stomach twisted in knots, but I followed after.

Mrs. Diggory was there, clearing some empty tankards from a table near the bar. She looked up as we entered. "Oh, Inspector Graves. Did you still wish to have the table nearest the fireplace?"

He looked over at me for clarification.

"Oh," I said, my face turning pink. "That's perfectly fine."

"Then yes," he said. "That sounds fine to me, as well."

"Wonderful," Mrs. Diggory said. "Come over here, then."

She set us down, and brought us cool glasses of water to drink. "The meal for the day is a roasted turkey with potatoes, brussels sprouts, and minced meat pie. Does that sound all right with you both?"

"Yes, that sounds good," Sam said.

I nodded as well. "Yes, it sounds delicious."

Mrs. Diggory smiled, and turned, heading toward the door down to the kitchens.

Sam's gaze was fixed on the far wall, his fingers drumming on the table.

I watched him, seeing the stiffness in his shoulders, the clenching of his jaw...

"Is everything all right, Sam?" I asked.

He flinched, as if surprised. He looked over at me, and a rather stern expression appeared on his face. "Yes," he said, trying to smile, but it came across as more of a grimace. "How was your trip? Did you find what you were looking for about your late husband?"

I had a familiar feeling, blinking up at him. Hadn't Sidney asked me very nearly the same question?

"Oh, it was a very nice trip," I said. "Getting a chance to spend time with people who really knew and loved Roger was comforting. It gave me a chance to grieve a bit with those who understood where my pain was coming from. We shared a lot of happy memories, though, and I came home feeling more at peace."

Sam studied my face for a moment, but I watched as his shoulders began to relax finally. A smile, a very small smile, appeared, and he nodded. "I'm glad you were able to find some peace," he said. "Having closure after the death of a loved one is important, and can bring great healing."

"That's very true," I said. "That's how I am choosing to look at it."

He gave me a sidelong look. "What about...well, you know."

"What?" I asked.

"The questions you were going to ask," he said. "The whole reason for the trip."

"Oh..." I said. "Yes, well...I think I was looking for answers in the wrong place. Or thinking there were questions that never really existed in the first place."

I waited, not wanting to say anything further. If I did, I would be lying, and I knew he would be able to see straight through me. Not that I was obligated to tell him anything, but it was easier if he just dropped it and allowed me to keep my own secrets.

He searched my face, and seemed to understand that was precisely what I was trying to do.

"Well, I suppose that must also be a comfort to you," Sam said as the footsteps of Mrs. Diggory returned from the doorway down to the kitchen, a tray in her hands. "You can finally put all of that to rest."

"I certainly hope so," I said, smiling up at Mrs. Diggory as she delivered some bread and tea to our table.

After enjoying some of the freshly baked bread, and accepting the proffered tea, Sam sighed heavily, rubbing the back of his neck with his large hand.

"Everything all right?" I asked, stirring another cube of sugar into my cup.

"Well...there were some interesting things that happened this week while you were gone," he said.

"Oh dear," I said, my eyes widening. "Something tells me that when you say interesting, you really mean something very different."

He gave me an amused look. "Yes, I suppose that is true."

"So...what happened?" I asked.

He sighed, leaning forward on the table. "You aren't going to believe this," he said, looking over at me. "But there was another death in the village."

I stared at him, dumbfounded. I'd been home for an entire day, and hadn't heard a peep. But more than that...

"I was only gone for six days," I said. "How is it something like that could have happened in the short time I was gone?"

Sam scratched his chin. "I imagine it still would have

happened had you stayed. You just would have learned about it sooner."

"I'm surprised Irene didn't call me and tell me..." I said. "When was it?"

"About four nights ago now," Sam said. There was a heaviness in his words that troubled me.

"What exactly happened?" I asked.

"Well...it seems the victim was coming home late from the pub. We heard from several witnesses that he had been there well after midnight. When we found his body, it was... Well, there is no doubt in any of our minds that he was killed violently."

I swallowed hard, my throat growing tight.

"If you don't want me to tell you, especially over a meal..." he said.

"No, it's all right," I said. "Unless you don't want to tell me."

"That's not it," he said. "The victim appears to have been strangled, with something akin to a chain, or a cable wire. Not only that, but there were bruises all over his abdomen, suggesting that some of his ribs had been broken, likely from a fight before his death."

A chill ran down my spine, as I tried not to imagine someone being brutally attacked like that.

"That's...not all of it, though," Sam said.

When I looked at him, I realized there were spots of color in his cheeks, and he was having a difficult time meeting my eye.

"What do you mean?" I asked, goose pimples appearing on my arms.

Sam rubbed the back of his neck. "This was something I wish I could keep from you, but I'm afraid you'll hear about it one way or another, and it might be better coming from a friend instead of a stranger."

My heart began to beat faster, and fear twisted my stomach into knots. "I don't like the look in your eyes," I said.

Sam pursed his lips. "Well...according to the same witnesses who told us that the victim had been at the pub that night...and there were half a dozen, at least...the victim got into a heated quarrel with another one of the patrons that evening. And that person was Sidney Mason."

His words struck me as if they were a physical blow. I stared at him, but it was as if I couldn't comprehend the words he was speaking.

Sidney? There was no way.

"Sidney isn't a quarrelling sort of man..." I said.

"I know, it surprised me too," he said. "I even went so far as to see if there was possibly another Sidney in the village that they could have been mistaking him for. Apparently not."

"What did he and the victim fight about?" I asked, both afraid and curious about what the answer could possibly be.

Sam shrugged. "That's the interesting part, I suppose. No one knows how the fight started in the first place. It seems they were playing cards with some other gentlemen, and their conversation began to turn sour. Soon, they were yelling at one another, making blatant threats."

"May I ask who the victim was?" I asked, hoping to keep some sort of unbroken image of Sidney in my mind. "Or is that classified?"

"It's been in the papers," said Sam. "His name was Wilson Baxter. Worked at the lumber mill outside of the village. A good man, when he kept his temper in check. His family's been living here in Brookminster since it was founded."

"I see..." I said. "I don't think I knew him."

"You may have seen his wife come into your shop," Sam said. "Though they were never ones to have a great deal of wealth."

He dipped his head, bringing his likely now cold tea to his lips as Mrs. Diggory returned with her hands laden with plates of steaming food.

"Here we are," she said, setting a plate down in front of me, and then the other before Sam. "I'll be back in just a moment with the gravy."

The meat was sliced expertly, and drizzled with a wonderful herb gravy. It looked so moist and tender. The potatoes were steaming, the skin wrinkled, the white flesh beneath soft and buttery.

Despite it smelling delicious, I had very little appetite after the news that Sam had told me.

"I'm sorry," he said. "Really. I should have waited until after we'd eaten."

"No," I said, picking up my fork and smiling. "It's all right. I'm glad you told me."

We ate for some time in silence. The food really was good, as was the gravy that Mrs. Diggory brought out to us.

Then the question that was burning its way through my stomach could be suppressed no longer. "I take it that Sidney is now considered a suspect in Wilson Baxter's murder?"

Sam clenched his jaw, his eyes glued to the table. "Yes, I'm afraid he is."

That was a blow. "It's just...so hard to believe," I said.

Sam nodded. "I know. He certainly doesn't strike me as

the sort. And the thing is, just because he was involved with the victim the night of his death, it doesn't mean that he was the one to kill him."

"Have you had him in for questioning yet?" I asked.

Sam nodded. "Yes, two days ago, in fact. We called him in as soon as we had questioned the other witnesses. His story certainly seemed to check out, but all of our suspects remain just that until the killer is found."

"And you have no idea who it might have been?" I asked. "No better leads?"

"As of this moment, no," Sam said. "We are waiting for the autopsy report from the coroner, hoping it might reveal some more clues."

It was hard to believe Sidney could have gotten himself caught up in all this. The knots in my chest tightened as I thought back to our conversations yesterday. He had seemed so calm. How could he be, if he was a suspect in a murder investigation?

It just felt...wrong.

I sat back in my seat, chewing the inside of my lip. "It's strange, is all..." I said. "I saw him last night and he didn't say anything about another death in the village."

"You saw him last night?" Sam asked. "When?"

"Oh, just before six, I think," I said, realizing what I said could very well be used in the investigation now. "It was shortly after I'd gotten home from the train station. He came by to drop something off, and – "

Sam's eyes narrowed. "What was he dropping off?"

"Only some bread he'd baked," I said. "And we spent quite a while talking. He wanted to know how my trip went." I shook my head. "It doesn't feel right. Sidney is always very open about the things happening in the village.

He and Irene always seem to know what's going on with everyone else. With every other death, we have talked about it. He was even the one who came to me to tell me about Mrs. Lowell's death back in July."

Sam rubbed his cheek. "It's hard to believe it's been almost a month since that happened," he said. "And yet, a month between deaths like this is far too soon, if you ask me. Every time we solve a case, I keep hoping this is the last time. I'm not sure about you, but I could certainly do without these sorts of investigations. I think I've seen enough death to last me the rest of my life, and then some."

"I do understand," I said.

"I think it will be best if we simply try to put this all behind us," Sam said. "Regarding Sidney, that is. As of right now, his alibi is sound, so we are investigating alternative routes. And believe me, it would pain me to have to interrogate a friend of yours again like that."

We finished our meal, and I spent most of the time lost in thought. Sam attempted some polite conversation after that, but it was almost impossible, given the gravity of what he'd said earlier.

"Thank you for lunch," I said as we walked back outside onto the street together.

"You're quite welcome," he said. "I wish it could have been for better reasons, but I wanted you to know what had been happening. There was no sense in your being unprepared."

"I appreciate it," I said.

Sam hesitated, opening his mouth to speak, but then snapping it shut once again. "But if I were you, I would not get involved in this case, purely because of your association with one of the suspects. I can understand perfectly *why* you might want to...but you shouldn't."

"I was thinking the same thing," I said. "To be honest, I have very little patience left for these sorts of matters. I think...I think it would be best if I left this to you."

Sam exhaled sharply, relieved. "Good." He glanced down at his watch, and then gave me a rough smile. "All right, Mrs. Lightholder. I must be off. You take care, and have a pleasant rest of your day."

"Thank you, Inspector," I said.

"And Helen?" he said, partially turned away from me.

"Yes?"

"It's good to have you back in town," he said.

I smiled at him, but it didn't quite reach my eyes. "Yes...it is good to be back."

"I wish I'd had better news for you," he said.

"As do I," I said. "As do I."

7

The more I thought about it, the harder time I had with it.

Sidney Mason...was a suspect in a murder.

So much for my relaxing first afternoon home from London. I'd come back from visiting the Gordons, with an already wounded heart. Having learned everything I had about Roger, I knew that I needed some time to rest when I returned. I wanted time to process.

Now, though...I had this new information to worry about.

What surprised me more than anything was Sidney's blatant omission of Wilson Baxter's death. I was tempted to write it off as having simply not crossed his mind when we were speaking, and assume that he wasn't worried about being a suspect.

I wanted to believe that even more when I realized Irene had also not contacted me to let me know about the death. She, like Sidney, would have certainly wanted me to find out about what was happening in the village. She was the one who always knew what was going on.

I sunk down into the bathtub, blowing bubbles with my lips, my face flushed with heat, steam rising from the water.

This was all too confusing...but what troubled me the most was that I couldn't shake the feeling that Sidney *could* be a suspect.

If I trusted him like I thought I did, shouldn't I have fought Sam tooth and nail, denying Sidney's involvement, insisting that there was no way he could have ever done something so horrific?

So why was my stomach so knotted? Why was I so frightened of that being the truth, instead of believing it was impossible?

*Anything is possible, really...*a voice far in the back of my mind was saying. *Just look at Roger, for instance. You were so certain that you knew him, and then you find out that he was actually a spy.*

I didn't like that similarity.

*But a spy is very different from a murderer...*I said in response to that voice. *Roger was noble, heroic. He died protecting his country. If Sidney ended up being a murderer, what is honorable about that?*

Nothing, that small voice replied. *Nothing at all. And that's why you can't come to terms with it.*

Annoyed, I yanked the plug at the bottom of the tub, and the water began surging down the pipes.

I knew that was exactly why I was upset. No matter how much I tried to tell myself that he was not a murderer, that he couldn't possibly be, I couldn't convince myself.

Uncertainty made my skin crawl as I dressed for bed, wrapping myself up in my silk robe. When I climbed into bed, I pulled the blankets up over myself, settled into my pillows, and stared at the far wall.

*Sidney couldn't possibly be...*I thought.

...But what if he is? That small voice asked in return.

There was one aspect of him that I simply could not shake. It was something that had stuck with me ever since I'd met Sidney. There was so much that I didn't know about him. I didn't understand who he was, not fully. I may have known some of his likes and dislikes, as well as knowing his interests. But he never spoke of his childhood, or his family, or what he did before he moved to Brookminster. He had never fully explained why he'd come to this little village, either.

In many ways, Sidney was still a stranger to me. A very handsome, charming stranger that happened to move in next door.

I slept terribly that night. My dreams were plagued with deformed, bloody bodies, hidden just behind doorways, or bathed in the shadowed alleyways of London streets. Laughter followed after me, but I never saw the killer's face.

When I woke, it was still dark. I couldn't stand the thought of going back to sleep, so I rose early, and busied myself with tidying the shop downstairs, hours before I opened it back up for the first time in a week.

I ate breakfast, though found myself avoiding the bread that Sidney had brought for me. I made a large pot of tea, and carried it downstairs with me, pouring the hot water into a carafe to keep it warm. I knew I'd need it to keep me awake throughout the day.

I was grateful for the daylight, and for the chance to open my shop. I soon forgot all of the terrible images from my dreams as I helped ladies look for new pins for their dresses, or ribbon for their hats. It felt good to be back at it, to be helpful, to keep my mind focused on other things.

It was ten minutes to three when I heard a knock on my back door, and my heart leapt into my throat.

"Is everything all right, dear?" Mrs. Georgianna asked as I packaged up her new hat that I'd fixed for her, adorning it with some opals that she'd brought to me that had once belonged to her mother. "You look rather pale all of a sudden."

"Oh, it's quite all right," I said. "I just heard a knock at my back door."

As soon as the words left me, there was a second series of knocks.

"Perhaps you should go answer that?" Mrs. Georgianna asked.

I glanced over my shoulder, and it was as if I'd been plunged into an icy river.

Sidney was there at the window, waving at me, smiling.

I waved, smiling as wide as I could, and then pointed at the box, hoping he would understand that I was busy and couldn't come to answer immediately.

He nodded, and to my dismay, leaned against the window, showing that he was happy enough to wait.

My heart was beating against my ribs as I turned back to Mrs. Georgianna.

"Are you sure you're all right, dear?" Mrs. Georgianna asked.

"Oh, yes," I said, tying the ribbon shut on her box. "Just a little lightheaded. It might be the heat."

"Oh, perhaps you are coming down with something," she said, frowning at me. "Because I thought it was pleasant outside today."

I managed to hurry her out of the store, assuring her over and over that yes, I was fine, and of course I would take care of myself.

"You very well could have gotten sick on your trip away," she said as I stood with her at the door. "London is a filthy place."

"I agree," I said. "Perhaps I did. I shall go right up and tuck myself into bed."

"Very good," Mrs. Georgianna said. "You do just that."

As soon as I closed the door, I made my way back toward Sidney, my head pounding.

I had never been nervous to see him, and I knew that I was being unreasonable by assuming that he was anything but himself.

I took a deep, steadying breath as I gripped the door handle.

Maybe he will say something today, I thought. *I'll wait and see if he brings any of it up.*

I pulled the door open, smiling. "Hello there, Sidney."

"Good afternoon, Mrs. Lightholder," he said, tipping his hat to me. "How are you doing today?"

"Oh, just fine," I said, leaning against the doorway. "Just finished up for the day."

"I thought so," he said. "I just finished up my jobs myself. I thought I'd come over and see how everything was in your world."

He smiled at me, the same warm smile that he always used whenever we spoke.

"What sort of jobs have you been working on this week?" I asked. "Anything exciting?"

"Well, let's see now..." he said, resting his hand on the toolbelt that was buckled around his waist, just like it always was. "I repaired a window for Mr. Trent on Tuesday last, and helped to patch a hole in Mr. Diggory's car engine, something he's been trying to do for months now, and I finally had a chance to do it. Aside from that..." he said, scratching his scruffy chin. "I cannot think of anything else important that I've done, no."

I smiled as innocently as I could. That certainly would have been a perfect opportunity to tell me about the death, even if he didn't tell me about his possible involvement.

I was starting to believe that he was avoiding it on purpose.

"So what about the week I was away?" I asked. "We talked about me a lot last night. What about you? What sort of mischief did you get up to?"

This was the last chance. If he had any sense, he would know what I was alluding to.

There was a flash of something in his gaze, but his charming smile grew across his face, his freckles stretching. "Well, to be honest, it was quite lonely here without you..."

He took a step toward me, so close that I could smell the sweat on him, as well as whatever soap he used. Something like mint.

I backed up against the doorway, and realized he'd very nearly pinned me there.

He laid his hand on the doorway above my head, and leaned in close to me. I could feel his breath on my face.

"I must admit, I am quite fond of your company, Mrs. Lightholder."

My heart started hammering inside my chest, and I was certain he'd be able to hear it. Before today, I knew that this closeness would have confused me. Would I have liked his flirtations? Or would it have frightened me, like it did now?

My fear is rooted in something far different from insecurity, I thought.

I ducked out from underneath his arm, moving back inside the shop. "I'm happy we are friends as well, Sidney," I said, pretending to busy myself with tidying up some receipts, even though they were already in an order I liked. "And I know I could never pay you back for all the help that you've given me around my home."

He slowly leaned against the doorframe, sliding his hands into his pockets. I felt his gaze piercing the side of my face as I avoided his gaze. "Is everything all right?" he asked. "You seem a bit distant all of a sudden."

"Oh, everything's fine," I said, laughing. The sound was even unnatural to my own ears. "Just fine. I simply remembered that I had some things I needed to put away before tomorrow. Orders, you know. Mrs. Orielle is insistent that I get these clasps polished and repaired for her by tomorrow, so I needed to make sure they were out in the open so I didn't forget."

"Of course," Sidney said.

I swallowed nervously, my hands shaking as I moved boxes around mindlessly, trying desperately to make it look as if I was doing it all with a purpose.

"You know..." he said. "I was out fixing Mr. Diggory's car...yesterday, in fact."

My stomach plummeted, and I had to grip the shelf I knelt in front of in order to steady myself. "Oh?" I asked, laughing again. "I was near there yesterday, myself."

"Yes, I know," he said, a slight edge to his words. "I saw you having lunch with Inspector Graves."

I froze. It was as if all the wind had been kicked out of me.

His eyes were boring into the back of my neck, and for a moment, all I could hear was the sound of my own heartbeat in my ears.

My throat, as dry as sand, wouldn't allow me to swallow. I tried to clear it.

"I – I was, yes," I said, knowing it made little sense to lie about it.

"What's going on between you two?" he asked. "It seems you have been spending a great deal of time together as of late."

He wasn't the first to point that out, but Sam had asked me to keep it quiet that I had been helping the police with their investigations. I wanted to keep my word about that, but was beginning to realize that people were likely making false assumptions about the state of our relationship.

"It's nothing like that," I said, getting to my feet and finally meeting his gaze. "We were simply following up about the last case I'd done for him. He's asked me to keep that quiet, as there would be many people in the police department who wouldn't take kindly to someone like me being involved with – "

"I see," he said, his eyes narrowing slightly, his smile faltering.

Somehow, the conversation had been completely redirected toward me. Fear pumped through my veins, and I felt trapped in my own home.

He knew I was lying. It was clear in his gaze.

I needed to get myself out of this situation. If he prodded any further, he might figure out that Sam had told me about Sidney's possible involvement with Wilson Baxter's death.

My heart lurched as the phone nearby rang, and I gasped.

"Oh my goodness gracious," I said, hurrying over to it.

I hoisted the receiver into the air, quickly pressing it to my ear. I felt Sidney's gaze on me as I stood there, my back to him.

"Hello?" I asked.

"Hello, Mrs. Lightholder?" asked a voice on the other end. "I was wondering if I could place an order."

"Oh, Mrs. Harriot," I said, nearly giddy with relief. This was the out I needed. "Of course, yes. Just hold on one moment, all right? I need to get my order book."

"No problem, dear, I'll wait."

I set the receiver down on the table where the phone resided. I looked over at Sidney, and shrugged. "I'm sorry, Sidney, but it seems I need to get back to work. I suppose it's the price I pay for being away for a week."

Sidney's eyes flashed, but it quickly disappeared. He grinned at me, and his charming demeanor returned, as bright and sunny as always. "Of course," he said, winking. "It's a small price to pay, though, I'm certain. Oh, before I leave, did you still want me to take a look at that loose part of the garden wall in the back for you?"

"Oh, would you?" I asked, grabbing my order book and a pen from beside the till. "That would be wonderful."

"It's no trouble," he said. "I will get back to that, and leave you to your work."

"Thank you!" I said, beaming at him as I set the order book down on the table beside the telephone, lifting the phone back up to my ear.

He waved, and pulled the back door shut behind him.

I closed my eyes, sinking down into the chair beside the phone.

He was gone...and I couldn't have been more relieved.

8

I quickly wrote down Mrs. Harriot's order, which was a stressful endeavor in and of itself, but didn't linger at home. Sidney's behavior was enough to completely put me on edge, and there was only one person that I knew I could turn to in a situation like this.

Irene Driscoll.

I hurried through the village, the sun glaring down on the street. Everyone else seemed to be enjoying the beautiful day. Parents sat out in their front gardens while their children chased one another through the grass. Mr. Trent was pushing his mower, keeping his lawn trim and clean. I saw Mrs. Bennet ride by on her bicycle, smiling merrily even as she held her floppy hat atop her head.

I wished I could have stopped and enjoyed their happiness with them. They called out to me as I walked past, some even asking me to join them.

"I'm sorry, but I'm in a hurry," I said, my hand on my heart. "I would love to, though! Save some lemonade for me!"

The tea house appeared, and I hurried toward it.

When I stepped inside, I was surprised to find it very nearly empty. An elderly couple sat near the back, enjoying some tea cakes, several empty cups scattered around the table.

"Helen," said a voice off to the side. "What a surprise!"

I looked and saw Nathanial wiping down a table.

"Hello, Nathanial," I said.

He opened his arms to embrace me. "It's good to see you."

"It's wonderful to see you too," I said, giving him a warm hug. "You have no idea."

He released me, stepping back and looking at me. "Is everything all right? You look distressed."

"Well...is your wife here?" I asked. "There is something that I needed to speak with her about."

He wiped his hands on a cloth he procured from his apron pocket. "Yes, she is, but she's laid up in bed with a nasty cold."

My heart sank. "Oh," I said. "I was beginning to wonder why I hadn't heard from her since I got home."

"Yes, she was worried about that as well," Nathanial said. He looked down at the tray on the table, stacked high with dirty dishes. "Well, you know, I think she would be happy to see you. It might be just the thing to cheer her up. Why don't I go up and let her know? Would you mind watching the tables around here while I go speak with her?"

"Of course," I said. "I'd be happy to."

He disappeared through the back door near the kitchen, and returned just a few moments later.

"She said you are more than welcome to go up, but she asks that you excuse the state the house is in. I think everything is perfectly fine, but you know how she is. Everything needs to have a certain level of organization."

I smiled. "That's not a problem. Thank you for allowing me to see her."

I headed up to their house, feeling rather strange to be walking upstairs without either Nathanial or Irene, even though I'd been there many, many times now.

Their house was quaint, and comfortable, with a worn, red sofa, and a dining table that held as many memories as it did dents and scratches. The kitchen was painted a soft green, a color that Nathanial was not very keen on, but Irene had painted each door herself, adding little details of flowers and ivy around the frames.

Michael's toys were tucked away in a hand-painted blue chest that sat beside the fireplace, silently waiting for him to come home to play with them.

I hesitated before proceeding down the hall to their bedrooms. I had only ever glimpsed inside the one briefly, and Michael's door was usually kept closed, given the mess that Irene insisted that he lived in.

Sunlight streamed through a crack in the door, creating elongated shapes on the floor in the hall. I approached it with caution, finding myself rather nervous.

I raised my hand and gently knocked on the ancient, wooden frame. "Irene?" I asked. "It's me."

I thought I heard a muffled cry of some sort from inside, which was followed by a nose being cleared into a handkerchief. "Come in, dear," she said, rather congested. "Please come in."

I pushed open the door and found Irene sitting upright in her four poster bed, dressed in an ivory nightgown embroidered with roses, and a matching cap.

She rubbed her nose with a handkerchief, her face pink, her eyes puffy.

"Oh, my dear, it is good to see you," she said, smiling at me. "It feels as though we haven't seen each other in so much longer than a week."

"I understand that," I said, walking over to the side of the bed.

"Oh, I'm as well as I can be, I suppose..." she said, sniffling once again.

I took a seat at the end of the four poster, sinking into the rather pleasant down comforter folded up at the foot of the mattress. "That's what your husband said," I said. "I promise I won't get too close, though." I patted her leg through the blankets affectionately. "Though I do wish I'd known before I came over. I could have had some soup made up for you. Maybe brought you some of the chicken stock I made a few days back."

Her eyes narrowed. "Whatever do you mean, dear?"

"For your illness, of course," I said. "Nathanial said you were laid up in bed with a terrible cold."

Irene's eyes widened, and then she sighed, her shoulders now heavy with frustration. "That man...I love him dearly, but what good does he think that will do?"

It was my turn to be confused. "What's the matter?"

Irene sniffled once again, rubbing her nose with the handkerchief. "I'm not ill, though I suppose I can see why you would believe that. No, we received some very troubling news last night."

"Oh, dear," I said, all of my hopes of speaking to her about Sidney and the murder investigation falling by the wayside. "What happened?"

Irene kneaded the handkerchief in her lap, staring down

at its lovely, pale blue fabric. "Well, it's something we've been keeping track of for a few days now. The night after you left home, I received a phone call from my sister-in-law, Nancy. She was calling to let us know that my brother was finally being released from the military, and would be on his way home within the next few days. Elated and relieved, I thought the news could only be good. However, when she called us again two days later, she was in tears..."

My heart twisted in my chest.

Irene's eyes welled up, and she dabbed the tear-stained handkerchief to her eyes. "When she went to pick him up from the station, the person she met there was a very different man from the one she'd dropped off. He was being escorted by another soldier, who had been ordered to see him home, as there had been some concerns about Nigel's... well, his state of mind."

Heart aching, I thought I might know where this conversation was heading.

"She said that when she saw him, she...she couldn't even recognize him. She knew he'd been in some difficult combat situations, but he'd always come out of it all right. At least, that's what he'd told her. She told me, however, that his face was scarred now, and the whole left side of it had become almost disfigured, due to burns. He'd lost two fingers, and he walked with a limp. She said...she said she had never seen something so gut wrenching in her entire life."

*I can't even imagine it...*I thought. *It must be very nearly as awful as finding out your husband has passed away...*

"He recognized Nancy, which was good. They'd spoken plenty on the phone, and through letters. But the soldier that had accompanied him informed her that he had become terribly paranoid, especially in the last month or so.

The doctors feared that his mind was broken, and that he was going to need special care. So she brought him home here to Brookminster."

Irene adjusted the blankets over her knees, as if attempting to collect herself, yet clearly finding it difficult to do so.

"We spent some difficult days with him. He's become obstinate, and paranoid doesn't even begin to cover how he is acting. More than once, he attempted to escape in the middle of the night, simply getting out of bed and leaving the house. My poor sister-in-law is absolutely beside herself, and it has positively exhausted us all."

She sniffed, shaking her head.

"And then there's all this terrible news going around about Wilson Baxter," she said. "He certainly wasn't the nicest man in town, but when we found out he'd wound up dead, strangled to death in the street in the middle of the night..."

She pressed her fingers to her temples, shutting her eyes.

"Nancy called me this morning, absolutely terrified. She's convinced herself that it was Nigel that killed him," she said. "I told her that it was highly unlikely, but she is insisting it must be true, because one of the nights that Nigel managed to get out was supposedly the night that Wilson was killed. And since there was no weapon, and he'd been strangled, so there'd be no blood to prove it..." she blew her nose into the handkerchief. "She tells me that if anyone would have been able to strangle someone like that, it was someone who was in the military for as long as Nigel was. And if his mind has really snapped like the doctors fear, then how can anyone know for sure whether or not he might have done it?"

I stared at a spot on the wooden floor, where a knot swirled gracefully, just catching the sunlight on its very edge, making it seem like wet ink.

"I can't believe it was Nigel," Irene said, a note of defeat in her voice. "I just cannot bring myself to think that my baby brother would have been able to commit such a horrific act, even in the mental state that he is in."

I let out a small, low laugh that held no humor. "To be honest, I understand that train of thought better than you know."

Irene shifted in the bed. "What do you mean by that?"

I looked around at her, my throat feeling as if it were closing. "Never mind," I said. "You don't need to hear any of that right now."

"But what if I want to?" she asked. "I'm quite tired of wallowing in my own problems. Perhaps I could help you with what's on your mind?"

"No, really…" I said. "It's not the right time."

"Well, now, you really must tell me," Irene said.

I picked at the hem of my shirt, debating internally. "Are you sure?" I asked.

"Yes, of course," she said. "I really would prefer to not think about my brother, and whether or not he…"

"Well, you aren't going to believe it, but what's been troubling me actually has to do with the death of Wilson Baxter," I said.

Irene's face fell. "You just got home. How could you have possibly gotten tangled up in all that already?"

"I didn't intend to," I said. "It was Sam Graves who

informed me of what happened, actually. Over lunch yesterday afternoon."

Irene gasped. "You went out for lunch with Inspector Graves? And you're just telling me this now?"

"It isn't what you think," I said. "Though I suppose I thought it might have been a romantic meal, too...But that wasn't it at all. In fact, he just wanted to tell me about...well, what's been bothering me."

"Which you said had something to do with Wilson Baxter's death?" she asked.

I nodded. "Yes. You aren't going to believe this, but – "

A frantic knock at the door stopped me in mid-sentence.

"Who is it?" Irene asked, leaning and looking around me to the door.

The door was pushed open, and I was surprised to see Michael step into the room, his eyes as wide as saucers.

Irene was out of bed in a flash. "Sweetheart, what's the matter?" she asked. "Is everything all right?"

She knelt down in front of him, laying her hands on his shoulders.

His large grey eyes, the same shade as hers, were glassy. "Mummy, they took him away."

Cold fear pulsed through my veins.

"What do you mean, sweetheart? Who did they take?" Irene asked.

He sniffed, much the same way she had earlier. "Mr. Hodgins," he said. "The police – they came to their house. We were playing in the back garden when they came out the door and started talking to him, and then they took him away."

Irene glanced over her shoulder at me.

The butcher? I thought. *What do the police want with –*

"It's all right, sweetheart," Irene said. "Were your friends all right?"

"Yes," Michael said. "Mrs. Hodgins sent us all home, though. She was really upset."

"Yes, I can imagine," Irene said.

A man, being suddenly taken away by the police...in the middle of a murder investigation.

That couldn't possibly mean that Mr. Hodgins was a suspect?

"Irene, I need to go," I said, rising from the edge of the bed. "I think I am going to need to speak with Sam Graves about everything going on."

9

My mind was racing as I left the tea house. Everything seemed to be happening all at once, and I was having a difficult time trying to wrap my mind around everything that I had learned.

Irene's brother Nigel...someone who had been completely unknown to me, was now a possible contender for the murder of Wilson Baxter. I couldn't be sure if it made me feel better, or worse about the whole thing.

On the one hand, I realized as I forced myself to keep my pace steady and slow, it would be a great comfort to know that Sidney was not the murderer, after all. An incredible comfort. My spine tingled with the desire for it to be so. On the other hand, I hated the idea of someone in Irene's family being responsible for such a travesty. It would scar her for life, and the way she saw her brother would be forever changed...

No, neither of them can be the one, I thought, my hands tightening into fists as I stared at the cobbled street. *It has to be someone else...for both our sake's.*

The police station came into view a short time later, and I was pleased to see there were no protests or demonstrations happening out front this time around. After the understandable recent frustrations over the anonymous articles in the newspaper about a murderer running around the village, I knew that the police were starting to feel a little overwhelmed by the difficulties they were now facing.

And with yet another murder, they were sure to have their hands full.

I stepped into the foyer of the police station, the sound of phones ringing and people talking greeting me as soon as I opened the door. The heavy, stale stench of cigarette smoke seemed to cling to every surface, along with the old case files and the thousands of pages of paper that filled them.

The receptionist sat at her desk, just like she always did. Her dark hair, which fell in thick ringlets, was pinned up at the base of her neck, but some ringlets fell down around near her face. Just like always, there was a cigarette clenched in her teeth, and a nail file hurriedly blazed across the surface of her nails, so fast it was very nearly a blur.

I approached the counter, the heels of my shoes echoing across the tile floor. My steps drew the gaze of a few other officers who were walking between offices.

She looked up at me, her eyes narrowing. "Is this an emergency?" she asked in an icy voice.

"I need to speak with Inspector Graves," I said, knowing the best way to speak to this woman was directly. All she ever did was dance around my requests anyway.

She blinked slowly up at me, not conveying any interest in moving. "...And?" she asked.

I glared at her. "It's quite important," I said.

"Inspector Graves is a busy man," the receptionist said, her cigarette very nearly falling out from between her lips.

"Yes, I realize that," I said. "Is he in a meeting? Or could I go back and see him for a minute to – "

"Paige, get a load of this," the receptionist said, leaning back in her chair. "Little Miss Love Bird comes in and thinks she can just go back and see Graves whenever she wants."

A woman with hair as blonde as Irene's peered out from another office door behind the receptionists, chewing gum smacking between her teeth like a cow chewing cud. "Does she now?" she asked, her eyes moving very deliberately up to me. She leaned against her door frame, crossing her arms. "Well, I'm sorry to disappoint you, but just because you are the Inspector's new lady friend, it doesn't mean you can come in here whenever you – "

"Excuse me?" I asked, my eyes narrowing as I glared between the two. "I am not the Inspector's – "

The receptionist snorted, turning around and smirking at the woman named Paige. "She might be his longest romance, though," she said, cutting me off. "What's it going on now? A few months, right?"

Paige laughed. "She's certainly trying to sneak in to see him as much as she can, isn't she?"

"I am not," I said, my face flooding with color. "And I will not stand for these sorts of rumors. If I say nothing is happening between the Inspector and I, then – "

"Then you ought to listen to her, ladies," said Sam's voice, which had suddenly appeared around the corner from down the hall.

He strolled out in front of the receptionist's counter, a somewhat bemused expression on his strong face.

The receptionist and her friend Paige both stared out at him.

"I'm sorry, sir, we were just teasing," said the receptionist, snuffing out her cigarette on the ash tray near her elbow, joining the several others that had been extinguished before. The expression on her face, though, with her arched brows and her darting gaze, showed that she held no remorse for how she was speaking to me. "It won't happen again," she said.

Paige disappeared back into her office without saying another word.

I, however, was fuming, staring down at the receptionist.

"What is it that you needed to speak to me about?" Sam asked, nodding back toward his office.

I fell into step beside him, the blood still pumping rapidly through my body. "I have never been treated so poorly," I said, knowing full well that he could see the blush in my cheeks. "To be so utterly rude as they were, I – "

"I know," he said. "The gossip that happens to get around this office can be...well, frustrating to say the least – "

"It's just not true," I said. "And for those women to be so bluntly confrontational..."

He nodded. "I realize that. But Rachel is known as a talker around here. That proves useful, on occasion. Other times, however...she just doesn't know when to stop."

"Clearly," I said.

"Don't worry," he said. "She's more bark than bite."

"But did you hear what these people are saying about me? About us?" I asked. "Everyone seems to think that you and I are some sort of – "

"Couple, yes..." Sam said, rubbing the back of his neck nervously.

We stopped just outside his office, and he gestured for me to step inside.

I did so, my heels snapping against the floor as I made my way to a leather chair across from his desk.

He closed the door with a definitive *click,* and slowly made his way around the desk, taking his seat in front of the windows, the blinds drawn. The sunlight was still trying to peek its way through the slats.

"Listen, I'm sorry that I put you in this sort of situation," he said. "I should have been more aware of what people around here might be saying."

I folded my arms. "It isn't your fault," I said, the color in my cheeks deepening. My heart squirmed in my chest. Had their words bothered me so much because I wanted them to be true? Or because I didn't?

"I will make sure to address their actions," he said. "This is the third time this month that someone has complained about Rachel's behavior."

"Third time?" I asked. "What else has she been saying?"

"Nothing about you or I," he said. "But I can say for certain that she is the reason why there is so much infighting between the departments lately. And it makes perfect sense, when I heard that she and her husband are having trouble in their marriage...I think she means to make everyone else miserable, as well."

I sighed, deciding it was best to let go of my anger. "Well...I suppose that does make sense."

Sam gave me a pointed look across the desk, but it was gentle, despite his intimidating demeanor.

"I'm sorry," I said. "I did not mean to make such a scene."

"No, it's quite all right," he said. "Sometimes she needs to be reminded that she can't bully everyone around the way that she does."

Even so, I still felt guilty. Looking over at him, it made me wonder how he truly felt about everything that had been going on between us. For one, I had been very nearly convinced that it was a romantic invitation when he had asked me out for lunch. I turned out to be wrong, though... and he'd wanted to talk about the murder of Wilson Baxter instead.

On the other hand, I'd caught him behaving rather flustered around me, especially whenever the topic of his feelings toward me had been addressed.

He cleared his throat, and I wondered about the silence that had fallen between us. What was he thinking about all of this?

"Now that we've put that behind us," Sam said, leaning forward on his desk. "What was it you wanted to see me about?"

It was as if the confrontation with Rachel had completely wiped away the memory of why I had come here in the first place. It took me a moment to recall why I had rushed over. "Mr. Hodgins," I said, my stomach plummeting. "I was just over at the Driscoll's when their son arrived home, telling us that Mr. Hodgins had been taken away by the police. In my mind, given the current state of the village, the only thing I could think was that he was being taken in for questioning about the Wilson Baxter murder."

Sam's face split into an amused grin. "Leave it to you to learn about that. Yes, we did bring him in. We dug up a piece of interesting information from some of the townsfolk.

We learned that the butcher and the deceased had a long-standing friendship."

"What do you mean?" I asked.

"Well, I suppose you could say that they used to be friends. According to Hodgins, they –" he hesitated, glancing over my head at the door behind me.

"You aren't going to tell me?" I asked.

He sat there for a moment, his eyes fixed on the door. "There are few who know this yet," he said. "But Mr. Hodgins and Mr. Baxter had been friends for many years. They grew up together, apparently. Both hard working men with gruff personalities. It seems that Baxter even lent Hodgins some unpaid help to build the expansion he had built onto his house after his third son was born."

"I'm guessing something went amiss in their friendship for him to be taken in for questioning?" I asked.

Sam nodded. "According to Hodgins, who was quite willing to discuss the matter, the two men had a falling out some years ago. Apparently, Baxter had been making passes at Hodgins' wife, and Hodgins wasn't taking too kindly to that."

"Nor would I," I said.

"So Hodgins cut Baxter out of his life. This was nearly five years ago, though, from what it sounds like. And according to Hodgins, they hadn't spoken since. He was insistent about that, and said that he knew others would back it up," Sam said. He leaned back in his chair. "I'm inclined to believe him, especially given the fact that Baxter apparently swindled the butcher."

My heart skipped. "How so?"

"It was something to do with a recent investment Hodgins made into a small mining company that has been trying to start up for some time. Baxter was apparently part of the deal as well, and had gone in with the man behind the operation. It seems that Baxter somehow convinced them to steal the money Hodgins invested, and claim that the investment had been lost to encourage him to invest even more."

"That's terrible," I said. "Just to get back at Mr. Hodgins?"

Sam nodded.

"He had no right," I said. "He was the one who was in the wrong."

"And he likely knew that. But his guilt was likely buried under years of fear and anger, and sometimes it is too diffi-cult to bring that to the surface. It's just easier to ignore it," Sam said.

"I suppose..." I said. "But that doesn't make it right."

"It certainly doesn't," Sam agreed.

"So I take it that whole situation ended poorly," I said.

"According to Mr. Hodgins, it came to blows. The two men had to be wrenched apart one night. Thankfully they were in a public space when they ran into each other. I'm afraid we would have been investigating this murder case much earlier otherwise."

"You think it was Mr. Hodgins, then?" I asked.

Sam scratched his face thoughtfully. "Well, he certainly has the motive, doesn't he? Not once, but twice. Wilson Baxter seemed to have a personal vendetta against Mr. Hodgins, and it was obvious enough that he was willing to go so far as to harm him in order to get back at him."

"But Mr. Hodgins doesn't strike me as the type of person to retaliate in that situation," I said. "He may be a bit stern, but to go so far as to kill Baxter?"

"What if their fight broke out again?" Sam asked.

"Is that what he said happened?" I asked.

Sam shook his head. "No. As I said, he claims they haven't spoken in a long time. But he could very well be lying."

"You weren't in the room when they interviewed him?" I asked.

He shook his head. "No, I wasn't."

"I see," I said. I regarded him with a firm look. "I thought you were so certain it was Sidney Mason, when last we spoke."

"I am certainly still not writing him off, given their fight the night of Baxter's death," Sam said.

"This just gets murkier and murkier..." I muttered.

Then I remembered something. "You know, I gave Sidney another chance to mention Baxter's death to me, even tried to prompt him by asking about his week while I was away."

"And?" Sam asked. "He made no mention of it, did he?"

I shook my head. "No," I said. "Though he certainly was acting rather..."

"...Rather what?" Sam asked.

"It's nothing," I said, pushing aside the thoughts of Sidney's bizarre flirtations that seemed more over the top than usual. His charm had almost morphed into a sort of pushiness that was unsettling. "I'm just beginning to believe that he very well may be hiding something."

"I'm not entirely surprised," Sam said. "If he was innocent, then it's likely the whole matter slipped his mind. If he's guilty, however...wouldn't you act the same, doing your best to cover up whatever might have been perceived as happening?"

"I suppose," I said. "Even still, this whole thing is

uncomfortable. The butcher? Sidney Mason? It just makes me think I'm living in a dark nightmare."

"I wish I could agree," he said. "My good grace is hard to win, as I have found it incredibly hard to trust anyone anymore. All people are capable of dark deeds, if pushed far enough."

"Such a hopeless view of the world..." I said.

"And yet, it's reality," Sam said, a heaviness in his words.

He sighed, getting to his feet and crossing to a filing cabinet beside the window.

"Helen, you are one of those few people I trust, which is why I have allowed you to have insight into these situations. I would ask again, however, that you be careful. I know that even if I were to tell you to stay out of this whole situation, you wouldn't. I know you'll go digging up information in a way that only you seem to be able to. So please...just be careful, all right?"

I laughed, a low, hollow sound. "To be honest, Inspector, I had every intention of sitting this one out. But it seems that the mysteries of Brookminster just have their way of entangling me in their webs."

He glanced at me over his shoulder. "I know," he said in a low voice. "And that's why I am warning you to watch your back."

10

My heart was heavy as I left the police station, and my head swam with questions. Not about the murder, exactly...that all seemed rather cut and dry. But I nevertheless found myself thinking about Sam's morose outlook on people. He said he found he couldn't trust people, and that they were all capable of doing terrible things to others.

As much as I wanted to rail against that in my own heart, to brush it aside, I couldn't. Not only was our world torn asunder by a war that was entirely out of our control, but the sweet, quiet exterior of Brookminster was nothing but a lie, when underneath there was a miry, dark underbelly that housed all the depravity that I had witnessed these last few months.

It was sad, really...and disheartening to think that the world was dark with only a few bright lights of hope shining in it, as opposed to a place full of promise and opportunity where everyone got along. But if the latter was the truth, then wouldn't we all be able to exist in peace, and not murder one another?

The world felt as if it weighed on me heavily, and I was not pleased as I headed home.

The truth was, there were still no definite answers about who had killed Wilson Baxter. It seemed that it was either Sidney, Hodgins, or Irene's brother.

I stopped in my tracks, halfway back to my house.

Irene's brother. I had completely forgotten to say anything to Sam about him.

And yet...did I need to?

Guilt washed over me as I realized I had considered betraying Irene's trust. What sort of friend did that make me?

But what if he had been the one to kill Wilson? Would she go to Sam with it? Or would she want to do what she could to protect her brother?

Did I even have a right to butt into the whole situation? It had to do with Irene's family. Was it right for me to take the information she'd shared with me to Sam, even if her brother was possibly the one who had killed Wilson Baxter?

I realized the best way for me to answer that was to ask Irene about it in the first place. She and I were adults, and she would have to realize that if he had been the one to commit the crime, sooner or later the truth would be revealed.

I anxiously made my way back home, hoping to avoid anyone I might know as I did so. I didn't want to stop and chat. I had one goal in mind, and that was to speak to Irene.

I noticed Sidney walking around the side of his house, a bundle of dead branches in his hands.

Ducking low behind the stone wall, my heart jumped into my throat.

He was the *last* person I wanted to run into.

I waited, hearing him whistling through his teeth as he worked in the side yard. I held my breath as the rustling of branches made me wonder if he intended to stay there for the rest of the afternoon.

What if he's waiting to talk to me? I thought. *Does he know that I'm not home right now?*

The tightness in my chest told me that I really didn't want to run into him. Given his avoidance of the conversation about Wilson Baxter, and Sam's suspicion of his involvement in his death...

Could I even trust anything that Sidney said anymore? I hated to doubt a friend...

But Sam's words kept drifting back into my mind.

My good grace is hard to win, as I have found it incredibly hard to trust anyone anymore. All people are capable of dark deeds, if pushed far enough.

It was grim, indeed. But what had Sam seen to lead him to that conclusion? What hurts had he experienced to make him so afraid of other people, of trusting them?

Sidney's whistling faded, as did his footsteps.

Now's my chance, I thought.

I hopped up and unlocked the gate, hurrying into my front garden.

My hands trembled as I fumbled with my key in the lock in the front door.

Sidney's whistling grew louder as I twisted the key, throwing my weight against the door. I threw myself into the dark interior, and hurriedly closed the door behind me.

I dropped down behind the window beside the front door, locking it behind me as quietly as I could.

Peering outside, I saw Sidney kneeling down in his front garden. A wheelbarrow was sitting up against the garden wall between our homes.

I saw him briefly glance upward, in the direction of my front door, but quickly return to his work, whistling once again.

I breathed a sigh of relief. He would have surely come to visit if he'd known I'd just gotten home. And I was not ready to see him right now.

I flipped the sign hanging just inside the window of my door, indicating that I was out for the afternoon and that the shop was closed.

Even though it was well past closing time for my shop, I hoped that Sidney might see it and believe I was indeed out for the afternoon. Though if he suspected I'd just come home...

He'd known I was lying the last few times we spoke. The look in his eyes had told me as much. The division between us was starting to grow, and it was making my skin itch just to think about it.

After being certain that Sidney was going to stay put in his yard, I hurried up the stairs, closing all the doors behind me, and careful to keep my lights off, even in my kitchen.

*I am going to such great lengths to ensure that Sidney doesn't know I'm home...*I thought, chewing the inside of my cheek. *I may as well admit that I think he could be capable of –*

But I couldn't even string the thought together. Not without feeling sick.

I settled into a chair in the kitchen, lifted the phone receiver off the hook, and dialed Irene's number.

It only rang twice before she answered.

"Hi, Irene," I said.

"Oh, hello there, dear, is everything all right?" she asked. "You ran out of here in a right hurry..."

"I know, and I'm sorry. I wanted to call and apologize for that."

"It's all right," Irene said. "But what happened to make you do that?"

"Mr. Hodgins being hauled down to the police station," I said. "I thought it might have been because of Wilson Baxter's murder."

I heard a sharp intake of breath. "Oh, that hadn't even crossed my mind," she said. "And...what did Inspector Graves say?"

My mouth was dry, and as I licked my lips, my tongue was like sandpaper. "Well, it seems that Mr. Hodgins and Mr. Baxter had a real history," I said. "Very old friends who had quite the falling out."

"I knew they'd been friends once," Irene said. "But never knew the full story."

"Yes," I said. "And apparently, Mr. Baxter just recently tried to swindle Mr. Hodgins, giving him motive for the murder in the first place."

"Oh my heavens..." Irene said. "Mr. Hodgins? Killing someone? I just...I couldn't imagine it."

"Nor can I," I said.

My heart caught in my throat. I desperately wanted to tell her about Sidney, but...something prevented me. Was it the uncertainty? Was it the fear of what might happen if Sam was right?

"I wanted to ask you how you were holding up," I said,

deciding now was not the time to address that. "I've never seen you so distressed."

"Yes, I am sorry if I've worried you," she said. "I've just had a terrible time with all this. Not only has taking care of my brother been utterly exhausting, it has been very trying on my spirit as well. He is a good man deep down, but I fear that the man he was died in the war..."

I sank back in my chair, letting out a long, heavy breath, staring up at the ceiling. "The war certainly does change people," I said. "If it's all right, may I ask what happened to him exactly? What caused all his wounds and his paranoia?"

"His platoon was attacked in the dead of night," Irene said. "A fire storm fell upon their camp, and he watched as many of his friends were burned alive. He was hurt, too, having gotten stuck in his tent when it caught fire. Then when he escaped, the enemy was waiting on the outskirts, and he had to fight them in hand to hand combat. He was one of three men who made it away alive, after having killed off the enemy patrol."

My heart sank as the images filled my mind. "I'm so sorry," I said.

"As am I," she said. "You can see the horror in his eyes when he thinks no one is looking at him. According to my sister-in-law, he relives it every single night, waking in terror, screaming as if he was being attacked in that very moment."

"I remember that..." I said. "Roger would wake in fear as well, though it was less screaming, and more gasping. He often told me that it felt like he couldn't breathe when he woke. It would sometimes take us hours to go back to sleep..."

"That's what my sister-in-law says," Irene said. "It's just so hard, because Nigel is such a gentle spirit. And he's always had the very best sense of humor." She laughed. "I remember once when we were children, we were playing down by the river, and he slipped and fell in. I expected him to be furious, as it was after a rainstorm and the mud had been all churned up in the water. He, on the other hand, to comfort me as I cried out of fear for him, pretended to be a swamp creature, growling and flailing his arms about...and then he slipped and fell in again. I laughed so hard, and he kept doing it, seeing how it made me feel better..." she said.

"He sounds like a wonderful brother," I said.

"He is," Irene said. "Between you and me, he's probably my favorite brother. He's always done things like that. Whenever anyone was upset, he was always there to help cheer them up. And now that he is in the state he is, there isn't anyone around to make everyone else laugh again..."

Her voice cracked slightly, and it made my heart hurt for her. It was discouraging to hear her speak with such hopelessness.

Why was that following me every step of the way today?

"Irene, I can't believe that your brother was the one who killed Wilson," I said, my heart lurching with hope as I said it. "I really can't."

"I certainly hope you're right," Irene said. "I've been debating going to tell Inspector Graves about our suspicions..."

"If Nigel becomes a suspect, I'm certain Sam will come to you with questions," I said. "He's quite thorough. I'm sure he wouldn't miss a clue that could lead him to the truth."

"Yes, I suppose so," Irene said. "I know that my sister-in-law is worried about it, too, though."

"There are some other suspects more closely tied to

Wilson Baxter than your brother," I said. "And besides...I think I have my own suspicions."

"Does that have anything to do with what you were trying to tell me when you were here at the house earlier?" she asked. "You seemed so worried about something."

"Yes," I said. "I was coming to talk to you about something that Sam had told me over lunch...the whole reason why he'd asked me to meet him out in the first place, away from the other prying ears in the police station."

"You sound upset," she said.

"That's because it's so troubling," I said.

I inched toward the window in my kitchen, the cord of the phone stretching out, almost fully, as I peered out into the back garden.

I could just make out the corner of Sidney's yard, the edge of his shed, and what looked like a pile of brush that he was clearing. I couldn't see him, though.

"It's about Sidney," I said. "He...well, he might be the one who..."

I heard a sharp gasp on the other end of the line. "You don't mean...Sam thinks that Sidney may have been the one to...Wilson Baxter?"

"Yes," I said. "And to be honest, I'm starting to wonder if he's right."

I retold Irene everything that I'd gone over with Sam. I told her about the fight that Sidney had had with Wilson the night he'd been killed at the pub. She seemed just as surprised as I was that he spent time down there. I told her about how he'd been acting somewhat strange around me, almost too friendly, and how he hadn't mentioned Wilson Baxter whatsoever.

"And I hate to even think it, given how he's been a friend to us for so long...but I just...I can't – "

Irene sat silently on the other end of the phone, processing everything I'd told her. At least, I assumed she was. She had said barely anything since I'd started talking to her.

"Sam made a very good point to me once," I said. "He told me that just because I didn't want something to be the truth, didn't mean that it wasn't. I hate to think that Sidney could have ever done anything so horrendous, or to think that we'd befriended someone who was capable of that, but..."

"I understand," Irene said. "But he is right...I don't like the idea either. Not at all."

We sat in silence for a few moments, contemplating the reality before us.

"We've been friends with him since he arrived," I said. "I've confided in him. He's helped with so much."

"He's been incredibly kind, and I feel as if he has gone to great lengths to create a very honorable reputation in this village," Irene said.

"But on the other hand, there is so much about him that we don't know," I said. "I have no idea where he came from, other than his accent. And I don't know anything about his family, his childhood, any friends he might have had before he came to live here in Brookminster..."

"That's true..." Irene said. "I suppose I never really thought about it like that. He is just so charming, it never really crossed my mind."

"But doesn't that bother you?" I asked, sinking back down into the chair beside the phone. "It's always bothered me. He's always been so evasive about it...changing the subject and turning the conversation back around to the person he was talking to."

"He does, doesn't he?" Irene asked. "Are you going to be looking into it?"

Fear washed over me like frigid rain. "I suppose I have no choice, do I?" I asked. "Otherwise I know that I won't be able to sleep."

Irene sighed on the other end. "I don't envy you," she said. "Truly, I don't. Just be careful, all right? If he was the one who – oh, I can't even say it. If he committed the crime, then that means he is dangerous. Try not to be alone with him, and whatever you do, don't hesitate to call for help if you need it, all right?"

"Right," I said, swallowing hard, my throat feeling as if it was closing up. "Yes. I won't. I'll keep that all in mind. I will be careful. And I will find the answers."

"And Helen?" Irene asked.

"Yes?" I asked.

"Take everything that he says from now on with a grain of salt," she said. "We should assume that it could all be a lie."

"...You're right," I said. "And I think he would be good at lying. Perhaps too good."

"I agree," Irene said. "So take care of yourself."

I realized I never needed her support more than I did in that moment.

11

I agonized over what I was going to do for the next three days. I knew I was putting off making any sort of decision, and I knew full well that there were quite a few people who were expecting me to follow through with investigating more about Sidney.

I considered calling Sam and asking him to find a superficial reason to search Sidney's house, but knew that he would tell me he would need some solid proof in order to do so. Getting the police involved would only be possible if I were to find something that could give them the justification they would need to break in and look.

Irene also called me twice over the next few days, asking after me, wondering if I'd found anything out yet. I had to tell her I hadn't, and found I felt a little guilty about it.

"If you want to back out, it's all right," Irene said. "There is nothing saying that you *have* to be the one to pinpoint Sidney's innocence or guilt. Maybe you should leave it to Sam – "

"He can't do anything, not yet," I said. "I can do this. I've done plenty of investigating over the last few months, this shouldn't worry me."

"Yes, but Sidney is a friend," Irene said. "That makes it that much harder."

She was right, after all.

I found myself peering out the windows of my shop every twenty minutes or so, looking for signs of Sidney in his yard. He seemed to be away for most of the day, likely doing odd jobs for those who needed him around town. There was no way for me to know for sure if he was home or not.

The idea of sneaking into Sidney's home sent tremors down my spine. Every time I thought about going inside without Sidney there, I recoiled in terror. That couldn't be the only way, right?

It was late one Thursday afternoon in early August, when I watched Sidney climb into his rebuilt truck, and head out into the village.

I had just closed up my shop for the day, and had nothing but a night of brooding ahead of me.

Now's my chance, I realized, and my mind went entirely blank. My breathing came in quick gasps, and the tips of my fingers began to go numb.

I didn't want to go. I was afraid. Sidney frightened me.

Why, though?

I had no choice. I had to go. I couldn't wait. Now was my best chance.

I swallowed my fear as best I could, pushed the thoughts of consequences from my mind, and began to prepare for my forced entry.

To throw Sidney off my trail, I turned on some lights in my shop, and maneuvered one of the mannequins in front of the window just so that from the outside, it could have easily been mistaken for me standing at the counter. I set a hat on top, and wrapped the neck in a shawl. It may have been too much, but it looked convincing when I looked outside from the garden.

I opened my order book in front of the mannequin as well, and turned on the gramophone so that music could just be heard from the back door.

Pleased with the appearance that I was, in fact, home, I slowly crossed over to the gate into Sidney's yard.

I realized that for all the times Sidney jumped over the wall into my garden, I had never once stepped foot into his.

It felt alien, and even though I'd seen it every day since moving to Brookminster, I felt immediately like I was intruding. Just like Sidney's past, he kept his own belongings secret, as well...which was why I had never been invited over to his house.

I remembered Sidney telling me that he always kept a spare key to his house in the back shed, as he was prone to losing his.

It was relatively easy to find. I found it on a simple nail hammered into the wooden wall just inside the door.

After a quick scan of the shed, I realized there was nothing important out there. It was full of tools, garden equipment, and spare car parts. I told myself I'd come back as a last resort to look if I found nothing at all in his house.

If Sidney comes home while I'm in his house, I need to have a good excuse for it, I thought. *What could I say that wouldn't make him furious? Is there anything I could say that would help him to be accepting of the idea, and believe my innocence?*

I chewed on my lip as I slipped the key into the back door, and with relief, I felt the lock give easily.

The house smelled like Sidney's cologne, which was earthy and reminded me of spearmint. He spent a great deal of time outdoors, and the interior of the lower half of his house indicated that.

His home looked very similar to my own, especially on the ground floor. The layout was the same, with the hardwood floors, the plaster walls, and the exposed beams in the ceiling.

His living space was down here, though. A worn sofa was pushed up against the wall, and a leather armchair was beside it, draped in an old quilt. Wooden tables were dotted around the room, but apart from that, it was rather bare. A bookshelf along the far wall was very nearly empty. As intelligent as Sidney was, though, I had always assumed he was a reader.

A beautiful wooden clock that hung on the wall caught my eye. It looked hand carved, with a little house atop the clock decorated with a green roof and intricately painted doors. A track spread out from the doors, and made me think that some tiny painted people would come out when the clock chimed the hour.

It was obvious, though, that there was nothing down here that could identify Sidney as Wilson Baxter's killer.

With apprehension, I glanced at the door leading up to the next floor of his home. More dangerous territory, as it would be impossible for him to not notice me up there if he came home, and even more impossible for me to escape without him knowing.

If I was going to learn the truth, however...I was going to have to do it.

I walked to the door and flipped on the light leading up to the next story. When I set my foot down on the bottom stair, it creaked underneath my weight, making my nerves sing with fear.

I held my breath as I eased my foot up onto the next step. And then I took another step, and another.

It was the longest trek up a flight of stairs that I had ever experienced, taking a moment after each step to listen, ensuring that he wasn't coming home at that exact moment. If he was, then I was caught, and had yet to think of an excuse.

What if I told him that I was just coming to drop off something for him? I thought as I continued my slow upward progress. *Well, that would only work if I actually had something to drop off. I should have made biscuits or perhaps brought him over some tea cakes.*

I grimaced as I realized that was a huge missed opportunity.

I finally made it up to the kitchen, my heart pounding in my chest. I flipped the light back off from the switch up at the top of the stairs, exactly where my own switch was located in my home.

For all the sparse decorating that Sidney had done on the lower floor, his upper floor was completely packed full of items. Immediately, I was struck with the sheer amount of boxes I saw. They were stacked everywhere, all along the walls, beside the ice box, even behind the door to the stairwell.

He had chosen to set up his home very differently than I had. He had no table in the kitchen, which shouldn't have surprised me, given the fact that he likely never had company over to visit. There was no sofa or sitting area in front of the fireplace in the living space, and instead the whole place had been converted into a huge office. An enormous mahogany desk was sitting in the middle of the room, piled high with papers.

What struck me most, though, was the cork board hung on the wall opposite the fireplace that was completely covered in papers, pictures, and red string pinned between them in a spiderweb of connections. Hand written notes were pinned haphazardly to it, as well.

My skin prickled, and I was afraid to even take a step further into the room. It felt foreign, dark, and enveloped in shadow.

Throat having long since gone dry, I did my best to keep myself calm.

This...this is Sidney's home, I thought. My footsteps sounded loud on the carpet, as my weight caused the old floorboards to creak.

The room itself was not as bright as I would have liked, and I didn't dare flip on the lights. But even in the dimness of the room...what I saw on the board made my knees weak.

At first, I was utterly convinced that I was seeing what my mind thought I wanted to see. Faces in photographs that had obviously all been taken without the subject's knowledge, some blurry, others taken from further away.

Names were scrawled on the pieces of torn paper. Names that I felt I almost recognized, names I'd heard before. Were they famous? Figures in government?

But then as I approached the board...there was a face on there that drew a gasp from me.

Roger. His face was on the board.

And not just once. Many times over.

It took me some time to realize that *every* picture had Roger in it.

What in the...?

My trembling fingers grazed over a photo of Roger wearing his military fatigues. The sight made my breath catch in my throat, pulling the air right from my lungs. How long had it been since I'd seen him like that? And not only wearing his military garb, but also to see *all* of him? All of the photos I had of him were from the waist up. How had I forgotten how long and lean his legs were? And the way he carried himself? It seemed so familiar, so lifelike...it was almost as if I could call out to him and he'd look up at me.

I stared at all of the pictures. Pictures of Roger, when he was walking through London, when he was at a pub with some other men, when he was taking a train...

A small sob escaped me when I found a picture of him and me together, in Plymouth, shopping at the market on Saturday morning. I held flowers in my arms, and he carried a basket filled with fresh produce and bread.

How...how had Sidney gotten this photo? I remembered that day like it was yesterday. It was one of the first times he had come home from London after the war had started. All he wanted to do was spend as much time together as possible. And not only that, but he wanted to explore and be away from anything that could remind him of the war.

But...

The questions that started to chase themselves around inside my mind made me feel ill. Sidney had all these photos in his house...of my late husband, and even...me?

My blood turned to ice as I looked over the rest of the board. The names I saw...I began to remember them, as they were all names that Roger had mentioned to me at some time or another in the past. Names of generals, of soldiers, of places he'd been stationed at, companies he'd had to work with since the war began...

I stared from picture to picture, each time astounded by the fact that it was Roger. It was really his face. His name. His identity, spread out all over this board as if –

My stomach clenched. As if he was someone important. As if his life was worth dissecting, tracking, learning the secrets of.

But he was. Hadn't Patrick Gordon told me as much when I'd gone to visit him and his family in London? As I looked at the strings connecting certain images together, I realized that there were, in fact, more people that were aware of Roger's position as a spy than perhaps even Roger had known. And given his position, it was no wonder that he was targeted the way he was.

These pictures were proof that his position was not a safe one, and just further proved to me that his desire to keep me out of arm's reach had perhaps been the right one.

A sound downstairs finally snapped my attention away from the board.

I hunkered down, the fear spreading through my limbs like poison, making my knees weak.

What was I going to do? If that was Sidney arriving home, I was utterly trapped upstairs.

I glanced around, desperate for a place I could hide.

I could bide my time inside a closet, or perhaps behind a piece of furniture that was large enough...

The idea sounded preposterous, but wasn't it the only choice I had?

I could just wait until he fell asleep, I said to myself. *That shouldn't be too long now, right?*

A creak of the stairs made all the hairs on my neck stand up.

I had no time. I had no other choice.

I dashed across the kitchen, desperate to keep my footsteps as silent as possible. It was a race to see who would get there first; Sidney, up to his flat, or me, into the broom cupboard beside the door to the washroom.

I managed to make it, pulling the door open and throwing myself inside. I was just dragging it shut behind me when I heard Sidney's footsteps on the last few stairs.

My heart thundered in my chest as I listened. A narrow beam of light peeked in through the gap between the door and the frame. I could only see a sliver of the kitchen beyond, but it was enough to reveal Sidney to me as he walked fully into the room.

I bit down on my tongue to prevent myself from crying out.

Stay calm. I can still get out of this.

I repeated that over and over as I watched him walk around the sparse kitchen. He pulled his jacket off and tossed it over his arm. Stopping at the ice box, he pulled the door open, withdrawing a bottle of milk.

He tipped it back, pressing the bottle to his lips, and took long, loud slurps.

My throat tight and my lips dry, I could only hold my breath as I watched, and waited...

Sidney finally replaced the milk back into the ice box, half empty, and let out a sigh of contentment. Perhaps I would have found it funny at one point in time. Even yesterday, likely. But seeing the board on his wall, and the pictures of Roger...the picture of me...

Something brushed against my shoulder, tickling the side of my neck.

I couldn't help it. A gasp escaped me, and I jumped

backward, landing against a broom...which knocked against the back of the cupboard with a loud *bang*.

My stomach plummeted to the floor.

Through the crack, I saw Sidney turn on the spot and rush over to the closet.

As he yanked the door open, I realized I had no choice but to accept my fate.

The light from the room washed over me, making me squint as I tried to right my balance, still brushing off whatever spider or bug it was that had chosen that moment to crawl on me in the dark.

Sidney's eyes widened when they fell on me.

"Helen..." he said, concern coating his words. "What're you doing here?"

12

As frightened as I was, my mind went entirely blank, standing there in that closet. I had no idea what to say. Or what to do. All I could do was stare up at him...this man that until very recently, I had been so sure I could trust.

"Are you all right?" he asked in his Scottish accent, leaning into the closet with his hand outstretched toward me. "You aren't hurt, are you?"

"N – no," I said, allowing him to help me out of the dank, musty broom cupboard. As soon as I'd forgotten what I was so upset about, it all came flooding back to me in an instant.

Especially when I could see the board over his shoulder.

"Well, that's a relief," he said, his charming smile stretching across his freckled face. "I would have been quite upset had something happened to you."

That familiar chill ran down my spine as I saw a troubling glint of something almost dangerous in his gaze.

I yanked my hand out from his own, my gaze hardening.

"You can drop the act, Sidney," I said. "I saw your board, and my husband's pictures all over it."

Sidney folded his arms and glanced over his shoulder. He regarded it for a few moments. "Yes, I suppose this could have ended in one of two ways," he said, turning to look back at me. The dark flicker in his eyes had returned, and a wicked smile replaced his charming one. "Either you'd find out, or I'd manage to kill you first."

A chill racked my whole body when I realized that his Scottish accent had completely disappeared...only to be replaced by another, much more harsh in nature, and thicker.

German. It was a German accent.

Before I could do anything, Sidney grabbed hold of my arm and dragged me from the closet.

"Let go of me," I demanded, trying to pull myself free. "Sidney, stop, you're hurting me."

He didn't listen.

He walked me over to a chair, where he threw me down into it.

Jostled and surprised by his sudden change in personality, I didn't think to react quickly enough, and so, he managed to find something to secure my hands to the back of the chair with. Something strong, like a leather cord.

My heart was beating so fast it was making the whole room spin. Panic began to well up within me, clouding my thoughts.

I have to get out of here. He's going to hurt me. I need to find help. I can't stay here. Sidney is not who I thought he was.

"You know, I should have predicted this would happen," Sidney said from behind me, tightening the second strap around my wrists much tighter than the first, so tight it made it impossible for me to move my hands at all. It squeezed so tightly against my skin that the bones in my wrists ached. "You have proven yourself to be awfully clever. I can see why he married someone like you."

With a jolt to my heart like a lightning strike, I glanced over my shoulder at him. "You knew Roger..." I said. "All this time you were lying to me?"

Satisfied with how he'd tied the straps around my wrists, he stood and walked back around to stand in front of the board filled with pictures and notes. "I had no choice," he said simply. "My own feelings about all this don't matter. It was a job, and I was meant to fulfill it. It's as simple as that."

My eyes narrowed. "It's never as easy as that..." I said.

"Oh, it certainly is, in my line of work," Sidney said, clasping his hands casually behind his back as he studied the board. "But goodness, you certainly have not made things easy for me, have you?"

"What do I have to do with anything?" I asked. "And why are you so obsessed with Roger? Why is his face all over your wall?"

"Obsessed?" Sidney asked, glancing over his shoulder at me. "Hardly. A great deal of this knowledge was utterly commonplace...well, except to you, of course. I have never met a woman who was so entirely uninformed on her husband and his business in my entire life."

My blood began to boil. "It was Roger's choice to keep me in the dark...so people like *you* didn't start coming around, looking for information."

"Is that what he did?" Sidney asked. "Huh. Well, I suppose it fits with his character. Self-righteous, as always – "

"Roger was *not* self-righteous," I snapped, my hands

balling into fists behind my back. "He was anything but that."

"And how would you know for certain?" Sidney asked, turning around to face me. He gestured up to the board. "Tell me...what was it that your husband did, hmm?"

I opened my mouth to answer, then snapped it shut. I realized this was exactly the sort of situation that Roger had wanted to protect me from, whether I'd known it or not at the time...and I was dishonoring his memory and all his efforts by spilling what little I did know to get back at a man who was not at all like I thought he was.

A smirk passed across Sidney's face. "I thought so."

He turned back to the board, and pointed at a picture of Roger in what appeared to be some sort of warehouse, with men in trench coats and bowler hats. "Allow me to enlighten you on who Roger Lightholder was then, shall I?"

I tugged against the straps around my wrists. The one around my left wrist was so tight that it did nothing but cause me pain. But the one on my right...it wiggled ever so slightly, just a fraction looser than the other. That might be all I needed to free myself.

I set my face, though, my jaw clenched as I realized he was going to tell me things I would not be able to get away from.

"Roger Lightholder was a specially trained spy in the British special forces. A man highly skilled in all manner of espionage, he was also trained in hand to hand combat and the competent use of any weapon placed in his hands. He could operate vehicles from cars to planes, and was fluent in several languages, my own tongue of German being one of them," Sidney said. "He was an experienced and shrewd negotiator, and given his size and ability to kill a man with nothing more than a quick snap of his wrists, he'd earned a reputation for being quite formidable. So, naturally...many wanted him dead."

My skin prickled as he stared back and forth between the pictures. I didn't know whether or not to believe what he said. Not to mention I was rather ashamed to admit that I *wanted* to hear more about Roger and his life, as I knew so little...

"Not only that, but your husband was also wanted for a very particular reason...something that he alone was a master at, something that no one could even come close to his level and skill in...he was a code breaker, which was incredibly valuable to British Intelligence. Thanks to Roger and men like him, the British could detect attacks and information quickly and pass that information along to their allies, thereby thwarting our plans in action, and ultimately, finding a way to get the upper hand in this war. As you can imagine, that was something Germany and her allies did *not* want to continue...and so a man as valuable as Roger had to go."

My eyes narrowed. How could he speak so flippantly about someone's life like that?

"Your husband managed to crack a code that I had been working on personally...it had taken him a great deal of time, but he'd managed to do it nonetheless. And do you know where he hid this code?" Sidney asked, his eyes flashing dangerously as he looked over at me.

All I could do was stare up at him. He really wanted me to answer that? But then before he spoke, it struck me as hard as it had the first time.

"My letters..." I said.

Sidney smiled at me. "Well done, Helen. So you did

figure that out eventually. I thought you might, having gone to see Roger's London friends. You never told me their names...Was it possibly the Michaels? Or the Gordons? Or maybe it was even Dr. Lilith Stroughbeck?"

I was not going to give him the satisfaction of knowing, so I simply hardened my gaze even further.

His smile widened, but never reached his eyes. "Very well. I won't bother them, don't worry. I didn't need to...not when I was able to track down Roger Lightholder's own wife."

He slid his left hand into his pocket, and pointed up at the photo of Roger and me with his right. "You were quite difficult to find. Roger certainly did a good job at hiding you. I suspect he had intended to feed you information through letters without you ever really being aware of it, as a means of back up, in case things ever went wrong...which they certainly did."

He walked over to the desk that sat in the middle of the room, and pulled open one of the drawers. It was filled to the top with papers, old newspapers, and bills. Sifting around inside for a moment, he finally pulled out a stack of letters that I recognized right away.

My stomach twisted into painful knots.

"You were the one breaking into my house this whole time..." I said, a heaviness squeezing my heart. "I was trusting you to watch my home, and you – you were breaking in. You shattered that picture of Roger and I, and –
"

"It may have been trespassing, certainly," Sidney said, rifling through the letters without care, ripping the edge of one, creasing the page of another. "But you cannot truly consider it breaking in when I knew where the key was the whole time, especially when you would often willingly give it to me for me to get inside so I could repair things for you, yes?"

The cold reality spread through me. He was right. I'd been the one allowing him in this whole time, completely unaware...

"And yes, I did break the picture of you and Roger. I thought it might be just the clue you needed to spur you on. I needed more information, and you wanted answers, so off you went to London, didn't you? Not that you shared anything when you returned home..." he muttered.

I'm glad that something told me to keep that secret from you...

"Well, regardless...Roger certainly thought highly of you, didn't he? He assumed you would realize that he had hidden the key to the code inside one of his last letters to you, and he trusted that you would read between the lines, and get the information into safe hands. But that's not how it all worked out...is it? No, it isn't. Yet there the code sat, in your possession, for all this time..."

"How did you know?" I asked, glaring up at him. "How did you know he'd hidden the key to the code in his letters to me?"

"Who else would he have trusted?" Sidney asked. "There were spies infiltrating the ranks of those he worked most closely with. How could he be certain none of them were aiding someone like me, someone who had successfully made his way into the country and worked himself into a position of trust? No, you were the only one he could have slipped the information to. You were the safe bet, since you were out of the city, and in some undisclosed location, a place that he never shared with anyone. Not even those he was closest to."

His words made sense, as much as I hated hearing them.

I waited until he spun around to regard the board once again before tugging on the straps around my wrists. The one on the left still constrained me. The right, however...was even looser this time. He had failed to tie the first knot as tight. Maybe it was good he hadn't really tried until I started arguing with him as he tied the second strap.

"You would have been fine, you know..." Sidney said. "Had you decided to remain in Plymouth. But no, you had to come to Brookminster and start your whole life over. You were the one who landed yourself in all this trouble. Had you listened to Roger's request and stayed in a safe place, I likely wouldn't have gotten to you before you figured out how important those letters of his were, and who knows where we all might be now?"

My throat grew tight at his words. Had it really all been my fault? Was my desire to move away from my past what started all this?

"When you revealed yourself in London once again, that made it easy for me to find you at the funeral. From there, however, I lost you once more. But after further digging...I realized you'd moved to Brookminster, where you were now living, working at your aunt's old shop."

"How did you learn that?" I asked.

Sidney smiled. "There are people in this town who are helpful to me," he said. "Money speaks louder than loyalty, sometimes...as do threats to hearth and home."

The blood pounded in my ears. "You're disgusting," I said.

He shrugged. "As I said, my emotions in this matter little. I don't care how you feel about it. It is a job, and I will see it through to the end."

My mind raced. Who could have been feeding Sidney information?

"Though I haven't needed my informants very much," he said, wandering over toward the window and peering outside. "It was rather convenient that the house next door to yours was available. Well, it was available when I ensured the tenant had been removed permanently."

I didn't need to ask any further questions about that. He made his meaning perfectly clear.

"I had not expected you to be so easy to woo, though, Mrs. Lightholder..." Sidney said, making his way back over to me. He reached out, laying a hand tenderly against my cheek.

I pulled my head out of his hands, snapping my neck back so fast it caused a kink in the muscle, sending shooting pains down my spine.

Sidney's face hardened. "Whether or not you want to admit it, Helen, you and I certainly have had our moments over these last few months. Which was perfect for me, and was exactly what I needed. You were easy to mold, sharing your heart when all I had to do was give you a smile and an ear to listen. I imagined you might have been starved for affection after Roger's death, but to easily fall into the arms of another man?"

"I never did any such thing," I cried, my cheeks flaring red. "There was always something off about you in my mind. There were things you never told me, things that any ordinary person would have happily shared. Family, history, childhood, memories of youth...any and all of those things were absent from our conversations. For some time, I just thought you were being modest, or perhaps someone had terribly hurt you, and like me, you wanted to get away."

He laughed. "Those things didn't matter enough to you. You still allowed me into your home, and trusted me. You *wanted* something to work out with us, you cannot deny it. I saw the flush of your cheeks, and the way you stared at me when we were alone. You were falling in love with me, and – "

"Stop it!" I cried, my heart beating so hard against my ribs it hurt. Sweat beaded on my back, and my hands were clammy and swollen. "No, I never loved you. Something always stopped me. And now I realize that it was my good sense, my intuition telling me to avoid you."

Sidney chuckled again, folding his arms. "Well, it doesn't matter, does it? Because my plan worked. I got what I wanted."

"Why didn't you just kill me and take the letters?" I asked. "Make it look like an accident, seeing as how you seem to have no trouble with that."

"Oh, I'd considered it," Sidney said, leaning back against his desk as casually as if we were swapping gardening tips or discussing the weather. "But I wanted to find some things out first. Namely, if you'd already sent the letters off to London. If you had, then my chasing you down had been an utter waste of time. I knew that would take time, and careful building of trust over these weeks and months. And as I said, my plan worked, because I've learned everything that I needed to. You knew nothing about the codes, or the letters. You knew so little that you hung those war-changing codes proudly on your wall, as if they were nothing more than a keepsake, completely unaware of the power you possessed. That night, when you showed the shadow box to Irene, Nathanial and I...Oh, Helen...you'd finally made my job too easy. You'd practically done it for me. You may as well have handed them to me that very night."

It was all starting to make sense. "You'd broken in several times before..." I said. "But were never able to find the letters. I'd hidden them away. I hadn't wanted to look at them myself. I had them stashed away far back in the attic. Seeing them had been – "

Why am I explaining myself to him?

"You should have left them in the box," Sidney said. "Had you, then perhaps you could have lived a little longer... at least until my patience decided to give way and I ended up killing you anyway."

"Why do you have to kill me?" I asked. "It isn't as if I knew what the code inside the letters said."

Sidney's laughter was harsh against my ears. "You expect me to believe that?" he asked. He picked up the letters and shook them in the air between us. "Roger was clever. He didn't hide the code in all of them, but only in one letter. The very last letter he'd ever sent to you while he was still alive. That letter was the key. It took me days, going through each and every one, until I realized...it was just the one. There may have been clues sprinkled throughout the others, but by the time he wrote you that last letter, he knew I was on to him, that I knew he had figured out the secret, and decided to take precautions in case he died."

I thought back to the night with Patrick and Lily Gordon, hearing Patrick's side of the story. He said that Roger had run into his office, terrified, saying he'd figured something out, he'd found the spy.

And the spy he'd found happened to be the one standing right in front of me, someone I had once considered a friend.

"All that was left was for me to find an opening to get the letters from you," Sidney said. "And once I did that, I could dispose of you. But in order to do so, I needed to find a distraction for you, something to keep you off my trail."

A chill ran down my spine. Sidney's tendrils sunk deeper and deeper with every secret he revealed. It became harder to breathe.

"I wanted to keep you busy, so naturally I had to find a way to do just that. You've seemed so fascinated by all these murders around the village over the last few months, so I thought it best to provide you with an opportunity to solve yet another one while I finalized my own plans on how to get in, steal the letters, and then find a way to take care of you in the process."

I stared up at him. "You...it *was* you."

Sidney smirked, folding his arms. "I imagine you were wondering why I hadn't mentioned anything to you about Wilson Baxter's death," he said. "Seeing how we spoke so openly about the other murders in the village."

"You killed him..." I said, and my stomach revolted. The images of the body that Sam Graves had portrayed to me ran through my mind, making bile rise in the back of my throat.

"I did," Sidney said. "And I suppose it was all for naught, since every time I had planned to try and kill you, you somehow managed to run off and do something else..."

"You've tried to kill me already?" I asked. "How? When?"

"It wouldn't do you much good for me to tell you now, would it?" he asked. "Come now, Helen. You know very well I can't spill *all* my secrets to you..."

He walked over to his fireplace, and grabbed a log from

the stack lying beside it. He set the letters down, picked up a box of matches, and pulled one free.

"What are you doing?" I asked, glancing from him to the letters, to the log now resting in the fireplace.

"I thought that might be obvious," he said, striking a match. It bloomed into life, a bright speck in the otherwise shadowed room. "This code key should have died with Roger. Now I can ensure that it really does. And my job will be done. Oh, at least, it will be after you are gone, too. Then I can return home. Finally."

He tucked the burning match beneath the log. Wadding up some newspapers from beside his desk, he set them around the log. Lighting two more matches, he caught the newspaper on fire. Its flames slowly began lapping up against the log, just waiting to catch.

He then picked up the letters again, and slowly turned his head around to me, smiling.

"Don't worry..." he said. "I'll read them to you once again as I burn them, so you can always remember how much Roger loved you...and how futile that love for you really was, in the end."

13

Sidney did just as he said he would. He began to read the letters that Roger had written to me, the special ones I'd set aside in that box. He read them with such tenderness, with such a gentle voice, the fire slowly spreading across the log, crackling as the flames consumed the wood.

I didn't want to give Sidney the satisfaction of bringing tears to my eyes. I looked down at my lap, my hair veiling my eyes, and pinched my lips together so they wouldn't tremble.

This was the most acute form of torture that I could have experienced. Hearing Roger's words read back to me by the man who had killed him was twisted, disgusting, and vile. It was wrong. Something so personal and intimate, between a man and the words he had written for his wife.

And with each letter he finished...he tossed them into the flames, where I could only sit and stare helplessly as the flames licked across the pages, devouring his words before my very eyes.

"...I hope you know that my love for you is as constant as the sun, as solid as the earth, and as vast as the galaxies. There is nothing in this world that could make me forget that. It is as strong as steel, as – "

I couldn't take it. A small, audible sob escaped me, and I regretted it at once.

"Oh, dear...is this too much for you?" Sidney asked. "I thought this might cheer your heart to hear your husband's words one last time. Besides, you'll be together with him soon enough. Isn't that great to hear?"

How could he talk about something so morbid so easily?

I didn't answer him. I just hung my head, not trusting myself to look up at him, terrified that I might crumble into a thousand pieces.

"Very well..." he said. "Then let's get this over with."

My head snapped up at precisely the moment that he threw all the rest of the letters into the fire, all at once.

"No..." I whispered.

"It had to be done," Sidney said, staring into the flames.

*I have to get out of here...*I thought.

I gave the straps behind me one final tug...and was stunned when my right hand slipped free.

I grasped onto the leather cord that slowly unraveled itself from around my wrist.

My left hand was still tightly pinned to the chair.

I carefully watched Sidney, who seemed to be relishing the moment as he watched one of his goals being fulfilled. He didn't see as I shifted my right hand behind my back, inching it toward the cords tied around my left wrist.

"I know you will never understand, Helen," Sidney said, glancing over at me. I froze, pinning my right hand to my back. "But I am doing this for the good of the world."

"That seems rather dramatic, doesn't it?" I asked, hoping to keep him busy long enough to be able to free myself.

"Perhaps…" he said, his gaze returning to the fire. The last traces of the letters were being swallowed up by the flames. "And yet…this is a moment that I have waited for, for quite some time…"

I managed to secure my fingers around the cord on my left arm, tugging on it as quietly and stiffly as I could, not wanting to alert him to what I was doing.

"Now…how should I do this?" he asked, getting to his feet as the last of the paper curled up on itself, charring, and turning to smoke. "You have been a good friend to me. Taken care of me over the last few months. Kept me company. I should not like to make this death painful for you."

All the blood drained from my face. I tried to keep my eyes on him as he walked away from the fireplace.

Tugging on the cord, I felt it loosen ever so slightly. My heart leapt. If I could just keep pulling –

Sidney was behind me now, and so I moved my arm back to where it had been tied, hoping he wouldn't look back at me.

"I could use some simple medicine to poison you," he said. "It would be utterly painless…as if you were falling asleep, slipping into a dreamless night. I could carry you back to your house, tuck you into your bed…and come morning, everyone would simply think that you died in your sleep."

"No," I said. "I prefer to remain alive, thank you."

"Don't we all?" he asked. "Very well, then what about a gunshot to the head? It would be instantaneous. I imagine you wouldn't feel a thing."

My stomach twisted, and the bile returned. "N – no," I said. "I would really like to just – "

"Yes, yes," Sidney said. "I understand. All right, well...I have one other option, but it's my least favorite. It would be – "

I tuned him out. He was standing down the hall, perhaps in a washroom or the like.

I used the chance to tug and pull as hard as I could at the cord around my wrist, and to my elation, it gave.

I was suddenly free.

Just as I was about to stand up and charge for the door, Sidney reappeared in the kitchen.

"I have these pills. Cyanide. I can't say it will be pleasant, exactly, but it's the same stuff soldiers have been using for some time now. They would have it in the form of a false tooth, and would chomp down on it if they were captured, so it would kill them almost instantly – "

As he approached me, my heart thundered in my chest. I knew I only had one chance, and that one chance might not even be enough.

He stepped in front of me, and I took that chance.

I launched myself out of the chair. With one motion, I brought my right hand around, curled into a fist, and it collided with the side of Sidney's jaw. He stumbled backwards, clutching at his face.

I had intended only to throw him off balance with the blow, giving me a chance to slip past him. Instead, I watched in surprise as his backwards stumble turned into a fall as his feet must have tangled beneath him. His hands clawed at empty air, finding nothing to catch hold of as he fell backward.

I winced at the sharp thud that sounded as his skull

collided with the edge of the stone fireplace behind him. I expected him to roll over and climb back to his feet. Yet, rather than fleeing, something held me in place as though my feet were glued to the floor.

I stood there staring down on him until it gradually dawned on me that his eyes gazing upward were not fixed on me towering over him. No, they were gazing sightlessly toward the ceiling. A puddle of red stickiness began to form beneath his head, quickly growing until it ran across the floor. Still, no part of him twitched or moved.

I knelt beside the body. With trembling hands, I reached out and pressed my fingers to Sidney's throat.

There was no pulse.

I'd killed him. I'd killed a man with my own two hands. It may have been in self-defense and partially an accident, but I knew that I would never be the same again after today.

He was going to kill me though, wasn't he? The pills he'd been holding in his hands lay some distance away on the floor, having flown out of his grasp when he tried to stop me.

The danger was over now, wasn't it?

It took me some time to gather myself enough to try and stand again. My knees were incredibly weak, and I wasn't sure they'd be able to hold my weight.

I staggered away from Sidney's body and struggled to get down the stairs, nearly tripping and falling, grasping the handrail as if my very life depended on it.

Drawing in shaky breaths, I grasped the railing, trying not to think about what had happened.

Guilt wracked me. Sidney's death was something that I could never take back. I had killed him...and I knew that would haunt me for the rest of my life.

And something else that was troubling?

I wasn't even sure I knew his real name.

He wasn't Sidney Mason, I told myself over and over as I stumbled toward the back door. *Sidney Mason never existed. The man that you fought with was a complete stranger. A dangerous stranger, and someone who was going to kill you had you not stepped in and defended yourself.*

It didn't matter, though. Devastated as I was, I could think of nothing else besides how suddenly he had gone from living to dead.

I tore out of the back door, letting it bang against the outside wall. It wouldn't matter now, anyways. The occupant inside wasn't alive to care whether or not the doors would be locked that night.

I somehow dragged myself over to the gate between our yards, yanked it open, and made my way inside.

Numbness was all I could feel. My blood pumped through my veins, and somewhere, far in the back of my mind, I knew I should be shattering into thousands of pieces, likely to never be put back together.

I found myself strangely calm now, however, as I unlocked the back door to my own home. The danger of being discovered had passed. And I had finally learned the truth.

I closed the door behind myself, shutting out the world outside.

There was one thing that was certain. I was going to have to tell someone what happened here. And there were very few who I could trust in the first place.

That left me with only one option. I had to get the information to the one person I knew who could help me out of this mess, and protect me from whatever consequences I might have to face.

He was not going to be pleased with me for having acted alone.

I walked to the washroom, where I washed my hands, scrubbing so hard with the soap bar that my hands quickly turned raw. The blood had never touched me, yet I imagined it tainted my skin.

I shuddered. It was going to be a long time before I was able to look myself in the eye again.

14

"So...Sidney Mason was not the man he seemed to be," Inspector Graves said, pacing back and forth in front of the window.

His dark eyebrows had knit themselves together in one, angry line. His jaw clenched and his hands clasped so tightly behind his back the knuckles had turned white, he'd listened to my tale of what had occurred at Sidney's home such a short time ago.

I realized as soon as I sat down in his office that there was a great deal of what Sidney told me that I could not share with the Inspector, because it had to do with my husband, and the military in general. I wasn't sure how much I was even supposed to know – likely none of it – but Sidney thought I was going to die with the knowledge, along with the letters he'd so carelessly thrown into the fireplace.

Sam glanced over at me. It had been some time since I'd spoken. My throat was hoarse from all the talking I'd done, and I was none too keen to relive the horrible memory again.

"All right, it's clear we have a great deal to discuss here," Sam said, stopping and giving me a rather hard look. "Let's start nearer the beginning. Sidney was not, in fact, a Scotsman."

I shook my head. "No."

"You say he was an undercover spy?" Sam asked.

I nodded. "Yes."

"And German?" Sam asked.

"Yes," I repeated. I had told him all this. Why did he insist on hashing it over again? Had I not been clear enough the first time?

"What I don't understand, I suppose, is why he was following you?" Sam asked. "You said he located you here in Brookminster and pursued you here, where he gained your trust so as to access information. About what?"

I looked up at Sam, slowly. My head felt as if it was full of lead. "I...I don't think I can tell you that," I said.

Sam's piercing blue eyes hardened like crystal. "It was about your husband, wasn't it?" he asked.

My eyes widened for the briefest moment, but it didn't matter. I knew he'd seen it.

Sam nodded. "Very well. I understand that because of his position within the government and the military, there are likely things you cannot share with me."

I shook my head. "I'm sorry."

"No need to apologize," Sam said. "Do you have plans to get the information that Sidney told you to those who need to hear it?"

I hesitated. That was something I had not considered... There would certainly be people interested in knowing that the German spy who had killed Roger was now dead. I just wished I had the letters to give to them as well...especially the last one.

My heart skipped a beat. The letter that Roger had written last to me...I must have read it a thousand times, especially after his death. And more recently, I had searched it for hints about his death, trying to see if he had sensed the end was coming, even before I'd ever suspected there could be a code written into the lines of script.

"What is quite astounding to me is that in order to distract you, he lashed out and killed Wilson Baxter. There was no motive aside from boredom or selfish gain. Surely he could have sent you on some wild goose chase instead of taking another man's life..." Sam continued, drawing me away from my thoughts.

"That troubled me as well," I said. "It was so senseless... Wilson Baxter never did anything to Sidney, but Sidney wanted his death to be a way to keep me occupied while he finalized his own plans. I suppose he thought that if I was too busy looking into the murder, I wouldn't have the time or energy to notice his scheming."

"Well, in that way, he was clever," Sam said. He shook his head, clicking his tongue in disgust. "He should have covered his tracks better, though. He was in the top three suspects for Wilson's murder."

"To be honest? I don't think he cared," I said. "I think he assumed that by the time you figured it out, he would have killed me too and been long gone with the information he wanted."

"Yes, I suppose so," Sam said. "What troubles me most, I think, was that I failed in my duty."

"How so?" I asked, brow furrowing.

"I'm an inspector. It's my task to discern when people are

lying, and are not who they say they are. Sidney Mason... well, I never thought twice about him. He seemed honorable enough, helping out everyone in the village. He always seemed charming, in his way, and no one ever complained about him." Sam scratched his stubbled chin. "Yes, I suppose that made for the perfect disguise, didn't it? Being so upstanding that he went entirely unnoticed?"

"And he was trained to do just that," I said, thinking back to the fact that he'd managed to infiltrate British Intelligence, entirely undetected. "So I wouldn't blame yourself for not seeing it sooner."

"Nevertheless...people's lives could have been saved, and in a way, that is my responsibility."

He resumed his seat across from me at his desk, and his gaze softened somewhat.

"I am glad, however, that you managed to find your way out of there unharmed. Not only are you able to bring to light the answers about Wilson Baxter's murder, but also the information you needed from him about your husband. And that could be worth more than gold in many ways."

"Yes," I said. "I imagine it could be."

"But Helen..." Sam said, his deep voice gentler now. "I'm glad you are all right. I may not have been there to witness what happened, exactly, but you were the one to make it out of there alive, and to have outwitted a spy...well, that's a feat in and of itself."

I frowned, my eyes stinging. The killing of another human being was not a matter I took pride in. Yet, I couldn't dwell on it right now.

"But wait..." I said, my mind beginning to move faster than I could keep up with. "What if he didn't destroy it all completely?" I asked.

"What do you mean?" Sam asked, his gaze hardening.

"Sam, give me some paper," I said, my heart starting to race. "And a pen."

"For what?"

"Please," I said. "Now."

Sam pulled open the drawers of his desk and pulled out a clean sheet of paper, pushing it across the desk to me. As soon as the pen was in my reach, I began to scrawl words down on the page.

My Dearest Helen,

How I miss you so. The weather here in London is less than ideal, with the winds coming in from the east almost every morning, bringing with them the chill of the winter sea.

"What are you...?" Sam asked.

I ignored him.

I kept writing. Writing and writing, as easily as if the words had been my own.

I sat there for nearly a half hour, during which Sam went to fetch us both some tea, of which I drank nothing. I feared if I lifted my hand from the page, I would forget a word, or misplace it, or misremember.

"There," I said, letting the pen fall from my now aching fingers, my palm clammy. "There may be a word or two missing here or there, but I am almost positive it's a very, very close match."

Sam peered at it over my shoulder, which I realized was entirely harmless, all things considered. Neither he nor I knew the key to the code that Roger had settled in between the words.

"I always wondered why this letter felt just a little different from the others he'd written. He spoke of things more poetically than he ever used to. After he died, I thought it was his way of romanticizing the world...but the truth was..."

I picked up the letter, folded it in thirds, and then looked up at Sam.

"Thank you," I said.

"For?" he asked.

"Everything," I said. "I never could have done any of this without your help."

"Oh, yes you could have," Sam said. "You did this all on your own anyway. I may not know *why* that letter is significant, but I imagine those who will want to know everything Sidney said to you will certainly be happy that it survived inside your head the way it did."

"I suppose I will need to return to London," I said. "I need to make sure this letter is delivered with my own hands. Who knows who I can really trust anymore?" I looked up at him. "Aside from you, of course, Sam..."

Sam's eyes softened, and he took a step toward me. "Helen, I..." he said. "Perhaps this is not the time to discuss it, but after everything that's happened, it makes me wonder...where this might leave things between – as I have been rather hopeful that something might – "

I held up my hands, my heart suddenly in my throat. "Sam..." I murmured.

I stared up into his face for a moment. His eyes, so kind, and so blue, reflected my own face peering up at him.

Sam was a good man. I knew that if things were different, he would have been the sort of man I would have been able to trust with my heart. Perhaps not initially, but he had proven himself over and over.

"I'm sorry," I said. "But I cannot think about those sorts of things right now...even as much as I respect you. I...I opened myself up far too much with Sidney, and I'm not certain I could easily do that again. At least...not right now."

Some of the light left Sam's eyes, and he looked down. He exhaled a long breath. "I understand. I'm sorry for putting you in such an awkward position."

I reached out, tipping his chin up so he could look at me once again. "You are a good man, Sam. And perhaps, given time, my heart will heal, and..."

He gave me a small smile before turning and walking back around his desk.

"Well, I do not wish to stop you from your inevitable trip to London," he said, cleaning up the pen and extra papers I hadn't used that were still lying across the surface of his desk. "We will all be here for you upon your return."

I smiled at him. "Thank you, Sam." And I hoped he knew I meant it.

He nodded to me, but then turned toward his filing cabinets, returning to his work.

My heart ached as I turned and headed from his office.

Sam was a fine person, and perhaps the sort of man I could fall in love with.

But those things would certainly have to wait. I had far too much else to worry about for now.

I glanced down at the letter in my hand. It was rather hard to believe I had been able to remember it...but those words had written themselves on my heart after Roger's death, and I had read them so many times I could have recited them in my sleep.

Confident in my ability to recall what they'd said, I set my mind on finding the fastest way to London...knowing that there would be celebrations and excitement waiting there for me.

15

I t wasn't even a week later before I was standing outside my front door in the bright sunlight, waiting once again for Irene's brother George to come and retrieve me and take me back to the train station, where the ticket in my pocket would allow me passage on the train to London.

The sun hat I wore had a wide brim, shielding me from the worst of the rays. I'd fashioned a black ribbon around it, tying it in a lovely bow that hung down over the back of the hat in an elegant manner.

It had given me something to focus on, aside from Sidney's death, in the last few days.

The trees cast long, dark shadows across the street, and the buildings themselves harbored cool alcoves in the alleyways between them, where the sun had not had a chance to reach. The Hodgins' large sheepdog was lying prostrate in one of these alleys, relishing the cool earth against his belly.

I did my best not to look over at the house next door to my own.

Sidney's body had been removed from his home just a few hours after I'd gone to speak with Sam. True to his word, the inspector had managed to smooth over any official repercussions for the death, claiming everything I'd done had been in self-defense. My testimony was found sound when they discovered the bottle of cyanide pills just a few feet from Sidney's body, along with all of the photos of Roger, though no one aside from Sam knew who it was. The rumor going around the village was that Sidney had been a stalker of mine, and that was why there had been a picture of me on that board of his.

I did nothing to deny it, of course, as it wasn't entirely different from the truth.

A movement out of the corner of my eye caught my attention, and when I turned to look, I found the street empty.

It wasn't the street, however, that had caught my eye. It was something sinking deeper into the shadows between two other homes further up the street.

A chill ran down my spine. Sidney –

But wait. It couldn't be him. He was dead.

I blinked, and I could clearly see the silhouette of someone standing there, and from the weight pressing upon me, and the hairs on my neck standing straight...they were looking directly at me.

But wasn't the man spying on me Sidney? I thought. I'd been so certain that the man I had glimpsed watching me from time to time had been the same one breaking into my house.

So who is this person following me?

I set down my suitcase and stepped out onto the street.

The figure hadn't yet moved, and so I slowly started toward them, my heart starting to beat faster.

As I stepped into the alleyway, the figure moved backward, staying well within the veil of the shadows.

This was the closest I'd ever been to the person. I had never had the chance to stare at them like I was now.

It was clearly a man, who was quite tall now that I stood so close. He had rather broad shoulders, much like Sam Graves, but he seemed more chiseled, and in a different sort of way, as if life had molded him to look this way.

And yet...something seemed oddly familiar about the way he stood there, staring at me.

"Who are you?" I asked, my heart beating so loud I was certain the strange man could hear it.

He didn't speak. He didn't move. For a moment, I wondered if I was actually seeing a man, or perhaps nothing more than the trunk of a tree distorted by the sunlight and shadows.

'All right, well, if you won't tell me who you are, then can you tell me why you are following me?" I asked. "And how you somehow seem to know my every move?"

The man still said nothing.

Instead, he nodded his head, just once, before turning around and slipping around the corner between the shops.

I hurried after him, wanting some answers...but was stopped dead in my tracks as a scent I had long since forgotten passed over me, making my knees weak.

I clutched the honey-stone wall beside me for support.

That was...

It was a strong scent, though very pleasing. Musk with a hint of woodsy, earthy greenery, like pine trees in the dead of winter, or the last grass of the autumn. It smelled clean, comforting, and...

Roger.

It was his cologne. I would have recognized it anywhere. He wore it all the time. I could never remember a time when he hadn't worn it.

My heart lurched, every one of my nerves suddenly singing.

Does this mean – no, it's not possible – can it be?

"Wait!" I called, hurrying around the corner.

The silhouetted man had disappeared.

I stood there, my knees trembling.

"R – Roger?" I murmured, clutching the wall.

I turned and inhaled once again, desperate for another chance to smell his cologne. It was much fainter now, but it still hung in the air ever so slightly.

My heart ached as I looked all around. Where had he gone? If that – but there was no way – why would he have walked away –

A horn honked, drawing me from my whirling thoughts.

George. It must have been George, ready to take me to London.

But – Roger –

If it was, somehow, by some miracle, indeed Roger...if it had been Roger this whole time, then why hadn't he revealed himself to me? Why hadn't he showed up at my house, ready to sweep me off my feet? Why hadn't he been the one to defeat Sidney, if he'd known who he was?

The horn honked again, and I hurried from the alleyway.

George was waiting outside his cab, peering up at the dark windows of my house.

"Sorry," I said in a somewhat shaky voice, trying to smile. "Didn't mean to make you wait."

He turned and smiled at me. "There you are. What were you doing all the way over there?"

"I – I thought I saw someone I knew," I said.

George's eyes narrowed. "You all right? You look a bit like you've seen a ghost."

I laughed, though it sounded hollow in my ears as I went to fetch my suitcase. "It was something like that, yes."

He helped get my things in the boot of the car, and then soon, we were off.

George began to regale me with tales of his latest trip to Brighton, but I hardly heard him. My mind was utterly focused on Roger.

*It couldn't have been him...*I thought. *It's not possible. He was killed by Sidney back in London all those months ago.*

Unless...that was what I was meant to believe. Was it at all possible that his death had been faked not once, but twice? Was it possible that he somehow managed to convince Sidney that he was dead, while also convincing many, many others of the same thing?

But why?

That much should have been clear. Roger's position in the military was one of great importance. Not only was he one of their greatest spies, but he was also a master code breaker, according to Sidney. Was it possible the government simply wanted any enemies off Roger's back so that he could pursue other vital, secret work?

If that was the case, then perhaps it wasn't that he didn't *want* to let me know he was still alive. Perhaps he simply couldn't, as it would jeopardize his mission. Maybe his brief moments of allowing me to see him in the shadows were his only way of letting me know that he was, in fact, still alive.

My heart surged with hope. Roger...still alive. Could I even allow myself to believe it?

Would this distance last forever, or just until the end of the war?

And not only that...but he had deceived me, and so many others, including his family and closest friends, all of whom truly believed him to be dead.

It left me with many questions, one of which was whether this meant our marriage was over or not.

Despite the questions, though...I felt an unexpected sense of peace, something I hadn't felt in some time. Not since his death, really.

If he wasn't dead, then there was no reason to grieve for him. And that brought me great comfort.

I settled into the cab, smiling a little out the window, wondering if he was watching me right that moment.

Through all of this, if I had learned anything through my investigations around the village, including this most recent one, it was that I had more control over my life and my circumstances than I had once believed. Not only was I no longer a helpless victim of fate, but I had found in my own way that I could make a difference in this world...just like Roger had.

And I was going to continue doing so for as long as necessary, for Brookminster was my home, and I was going to help protect it. I no longer had to run from my past, and though I wasn't sure what the future might hold, I was determined to make it a bright one.

～

Continue following the mysterious adventures of Helen
Lightholder in
"A Simple Country Killing."

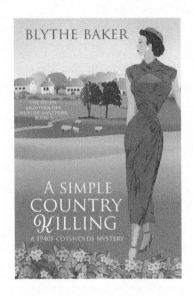

ABOUT THE AUTHOR

Blythe Baker is the lead writer behind several popular historical and paranormal mystery serieses. When Blythe isn't buried under clues, suspects, and motives, she's acting as chauffeur to her children and head groomer to her household of beloved pets. She enjoys walking her dog, lounging in her backyard hammock, and fiddling with graphic design. She also likes binge-watching mystery shows on TV.

To learn more about Blythe, visit her website and sign up for her newsletter at www.blythebaker.com